Unfinished Goodbyes

Unfinished Goodbyes

By: Blake Collins

Unfinished Goodbyes

ISBN: 979-8-9936801-0-1

Cover design by Blake Collins

Interior design by Blake Collins

Published by Blake Collins

Idaho Falls, Idaho

Printed in the United States of America

First Printing - 2025

To my amazing wife - whose love and faith carried me when I didn't believe in myself

Blake Collins

"What is grief, if not love persevering?"
— *WandaVision*

Blake Collins

Table of Contents

Table of Contents Cont.

Chapter 1 – A Distant Echo

Glass shatters. Screams. Her voice—

"Patrick!"

Headlights. The world tilts. Then silence.

I jolt awake, drenched in sweat, heart pounding. Basement ceiling. Darkness pressing in. For a second, I swear I still hear her.

Jessi.

I close my eyes, try to hold onto the sound. Her laugh. That dumb grin when she called me *Patch.* The way she could make fun of me and still make me feel like I mattered.

But it always fades. It always ends with the crash.

12:01 A.M.

Wide awake. Again.

The basement is cold. Silent. No photos of her down here. No reminders. Just the hum of my console in the corner, glowing like it knows I'll never sleep.

I clutch my pillow, legs twitching under the blanket. Breathing jagged, lungs fighting against the quiet. His voice plays on a loop in my head—
What did you do? You had one job.

Tomorrow starts senior year. My last nine months at Black Hills High. My last nine months of being invisible.

Except to him.

David Bell.

Quarterback. Town hero. If smugness wore cleats, it would look just like him. Everyone worships him—teachers, parents, the entire school. Dating Aliza Gillespie, captain of the cheerleaders. State champ. Untouchable.

And me? His favorite target.

Tomorrow, he'll slam into me in the hallway, call me loser, and send my books flying while his pack of shadows laughs. And I'll wait until they're gone. Wait until Elliot helps me pick everything up.

Elliot always helps.

Elliot Baldwin—best friend since kindergarten. Class clown. Short blonde hair, goofy smile, endless jokes. He lost both parents in a car crash when we were kids, and somehow he still makes life better for everyone else.

I don't know how he does it.

Me? I can't even sleep without seeing headlights.

12:18 A.M.

The silence buzzes. Too loud.

Close my eyes—whispers. Echoes. My own heart pounding like it's sprinting.

The room is cold, but sweat clings to me. My chest tightens, straw-thin breaths.

Blanket off. Blanket on. Air heavy. Shadows crawl across the wall every time I blink.

Throat dry. I stumble up, drink water, sit back down. Stare at nothing.

When it gets this bad, I try to hold her voice. Jessi—laughing. Tossing a pillow at me. Calling my room a mix of Cheetos and dirty socks. Telling me I needed a girlfriend who could clean.

Back then, her room was next to mine. Not this dungeon I used to be too scared to enter alone.

She called me *Patch*. Short for Patrick. Always with that grin, like it was an inside joke only she understood.

That stupid nickname used to make me furious.

Now? I'd give anything to hear it one more time.

I squeeze my eyes shut. Fight to trap her voice. If I can hold it tight enough, maybe she won't be gone.

But it always fades.

And when it does—
all that's left is the pounding in my head,
the ache in my chest,
and the echo of my own breath.

12:23 A.M.

How do people do it? Just… switch off?

Shut down their brains. Stop the sorrow. Silence the regret. Smother the voices. Sleep.

Two hours in bed and I haven't closed my eyes for more than ten seconds.

Tomorrow is coming. The first day of senior year. And I can already feel it pressing down. Crushing.

Every breath feels like it might be the last. Drowning. No air left. Just weight.

I used to have someone to talk to.

Mom.

Snacks after school. Homework help. Awkward advice about girls. She was always there. Always present.

That was before *the incident.*

Now? She's gone without leaving. Lost in Chardonnay. Glass after glass. Passed out on the couch before I can get a word out. Empty bottles on the floor. Empty glass on the table. Empty eyes when she does look at me.

Dad's different. The "ideal man." Football, baseball, track. Law school at USC. Linebacker. Almost NFL before his knee exploded.

Now he's an executive at Export Capital. Big job. Big expectations.

And me?

Not him. Not even close.

He yells every day. *Put down that book. Go outside. Don't you have any friends?*

He used to ask about my future. Girls. College. What I wanted to do.

I told him software design. Maybe video games. Something creative.

He laughed. No—he yelled. *Quit dreaming. You'll never get a job playing games. Get your head out of the clouds. Be realistic.*

But if it's not his way, it's wrong.

And if I'm not him, I'm nothing.

12:57 A.M.

I have to sleep. No—*need* to.

Alarm's set. Little more than five hours. Shower. Wash the grease from my black hair. Throw something clean on. Survive the most exciting day of the year—first day of school.

The bus comes at 6:30. Mom won't drive me. Not because she can't. Because she won't.

I used to drive myself. Before the accident. But the car didn't survive. Neither did their trust.

They won't even talk about replacing it. Too scared, maybe. Too sure I'll end up in a ditch again—with more than twisted metal this time. And I don't have the money to buy my own.

So if I miss the bus, I walk. If I walk, I'm late. Another perfect start to another perfect year.

I close my eyes. Beg them to stay closed. Beg the silence to wrap around me like a blanket. To keep the memories out.

I just want to rest. To stop reliving everything I lost.

But I know better.

School is looming. David's smirk already waiting in the hallway. The nightmare already crawling in.

It always comes—when I'm stressed, when I'm exhausted, when I think I might finally be okay.

It creeps in like fog through a cracked window. Like an unstoppable shadow swallowing me whole.

It's coming tonight. I can feel it.

Because no matter how hard I try to forget—
I can't.

I will never forget.

And that's the worst part.

Chapter 2 – The Place I Can't Escape

"This is Mix 96, and you're listening to today's Top 20 countdown…"

The radio hums in the background.

First week of summer vacation. Sun streaking across the windshield like gold ribbons. Jessi's beside me, blonde hair whipping out the passenger window, her voice cracking as she belts the wrong lyrics at the top of her lungs. She's laughing, alive, untouchable.

It's a perfect June day—the kind you wish you could trap in a snow globe and never let melt.

"I love elephants," she says suddenly, like we've been in that conversation all along. "They're so majestic. Huge, but gentle. There's just… something about them."

I snort. "That's random."

"We're going to the zoo, Patch," she grins. "It's our last hurrah, remember?"

"You're not even singing the right words," I tease.

"That's the point, Patch." She smirks. "Besides, I sound amazing. Admit it."

"The elephants might cry when they hear you."

"Good. More drama at the zoo. I'm here for it."

She kicks a flip-flop onto the dash, leaning back, glowing. Jessi was always like that—magnetic, like the sun could only shine brighter around her. Fifteen going on thirty. Class president. Cheerleader. Everyone's favorite.

And somehow, still my best friend.

"I still can't believe you're a senior next year," she says. "Does it feel weird?"

I shrug. "Weird… and pointless."

"You're so dramatic." She laughs. "You're going to regret not enjoying it."

"You think I'm going to enjoy senior year?"

"I think you could. If you stopped hiding behind your books and video games."

I'm about to fire back when the light ahead flashes red. Too late.

"Patrick!"

Her voice tears through me. My foot slams the brake. Tires scream.

The world jerks forward.

6:00 A.M.

The alarm clock is shrieking. My chest is heaving. Sheets drenched in sweat.

The dream. Again. Louder this time. Clearer.

I smelled the burnt rubber. I felt the blood.

Three months gone. But Jessi is still dying in my head.

All I'm left with is a scream. A crash. Silence.

An unfinished goodbye.

Shower. Steam fogs the mirror, but it doesn't wash away the weight pressing down on my chest.

Black t-shirt. Jeans. Nothing flashy. Mom said to wear something nice. But I don't want to be seen. I want to disappear.

6:19 A.M.

"Patrick, get out here!" Mom's voice slices through the floorboards. "The bus will be here in ten minutes. If you miss it, you're walking!"

"I KNOW, MOM!" I snap, sharper than I mean.

I hate mornings. I hate this one more than most.

Upstairs, Dad's at the table with his black coffee and his paper. Mom's in her robe with her first cup of the day—the one that keeps her stomach steady before the wine takes over.

Dad doesn't look up. Doesn't speak. His knuckles go pale around the mug.

He hasn't looked at me the same since the accident. Maybe he never will.

6:30 A.M.

Beep. Beep.

The bus horn. I grab my bag.

"Patrick—" Mom starts.

"Bus is here," I cut her off, slamming the door.

She was going to say it again. *He doesn't blame you.*

But it's a lie.

Everyone blames me.

Especially me.

The bus driver scowls as I climb on. "Try being on time, Schwartz."

I drop into my usual seat in the back. Jessi's seat. Our seat.

And the words echo anyway, louder than the driver's, louder than my mom's:

He does blame you.

Because he does.

Because they all do.

And the worst part is…
they're probably right.

Chapter 3 – Invisible Ink

The bus screeches to a stop in front of Black Hills High. Same brick walls. Same cracked sidewalk. Same peeling paint on the gym doors.

Above the entrance, the faded sign still reads:

Black Hills High School
Est. 1906 – Home of the Phantoms

Might as well say: *Welcome Back to Purgatory.*

I step off the bus. Elliot's already there, leaning against the bike rack like always. He waves me over, grin wide, energy buzzing. His grandparents let him drive the Jeep that once belonged to his dad; freedom wrapped in rust and squeaky shocks.

Around us, kids swarm like ants spilling from a kicked mound.
Freshmen wide-eyed.
Sophomores trying too hard.
Juniors fading into the background.
Seniors—fake confidence dripping from every forced laugh.

I don't belong to any of them.

Eyes slide past me, or linger just long enough to sting. A whisper rides the air: *That's him. The one who killed his sister.*

The rumor never had to be spoken. It just stuck.

"Schedule this year?" Elliot asks, dragging me back.

"English with Carson. Then History, Calc, Psych, Spanish IV, Graphic Design, Newspaper."

"Nice. We'll have Psych and Spanish together."

The bell cuts him off. Senior year officially begins.

Inside, it's chaos. Elbows. Shoving. Perfume, sweat, nerves. The lights too bright, the air too heavy. My head buzzes—could be the bleach, could be the panic.

I keep my eyes on the floor and slip into the back of Mrs. Carson's room. Just before the tardy bell.

Packets wait on every desk—thick rules stapled together like shackles.

Page 2, Rule 6: *No phones or electronics. Confiscation required.*

Powell's masterpiece. Principal by title, puppet by design. He keeps parents happy, teachers quiet, students pretending. Nothing more.

Mrs. Carson reads every word, her voice patient, steady. I don't hear half of it. Just the tick of the clock.
Tick.
Tick.
Tick.

The bell rings. The room empties in seconds. I wait. Always wait. The quiet feels safer.

"Patrick?"

Her voice stops me at the door.

I turn. Mrs. Carson steps closer, eyes soft.

"I'm glad you're in my homeroom this year."

"Yeah. Me too."

She hesitates, then lowers her voice.
"I just want you to know—I'm sorry. I know you probably hear that a lot, but… I'm here. If you ever need someone, I'm here."

For a second, something catches in my throat. Not words. Just… the possibility she means it.

"Thanks," I manage.

She smiles—gentle, unforced.

Mrs. Carson is one of the only teachers who ever saw me. Even before the accident. She still does. And I hate that it almost matters.

I step into the hall. The noise swallows me whole. Lockers slam. Shoes squeak. Laughter cuts sharp.

The thread of her voice breaks.

I pull up my hood. Drop my head.
Invisible again.

Blake Collins

Chapter 4 – The Mask He Wears

The hallway funnels us forward like cattle—one long, tangled mess of students pushing through narrow spaces and pretending to have somewhere important to be.

I keep my head down. Hood up. Books clutched tight. The goal is simple: survive until lunch.

I pass classroom after classroom, eyes fixed on the floor tiles. The voices around me blur into one long hum of gossip and gum-chewing.

I don't see him coming.

SLAM.

A wall of muscle crashes into my shoulder like a linebacker on a mission. My books explode across the floor. The hallway ripples with laughter.

"Watch where you're going, *loser,*" a familiar voice says, full of venom and victory.

David Bell.

Of course.

I kneel down, scrambling to collect my things. Before I can finish, a boot sweeps in and kicks my binder down the hallway. Another round of laughter erupts.

I clench my fists. My knuckles turn white. My vision blurs.

I want to hit him. Just once. I want him to bleed.

But I don't. I stay frozen—like always.

A teacher steps into the hall. David's voice shifts instantly.

"He dropped his books," he says with a perfect smile. "We were just trying to help."

"Thanks for being such a good friend, David," the teacher replies, completely unaware.

They all walk away laughing. Like it's a joke. Like I'm the joke.

I gather my books again and disappear into the rest of my schedule—Psychology, Graphic Design, and Writing for the school paper. Same old first-day speeches. Same fake smiles.

At 2:25, the bell rings. One day down. One hundred seventy-nine to go.

As I walk out the front doors, the sunlight is too bright. Too cheerful for how I feel.

I head toward the bus, ready to vanish into my basement again. But then—

Chapter 5 – Bittersweet

As I head out the door, the light is blinding from the warmth, on the last day in August. I'm going to miss those days. I hate the cold and the snow. If I could wear a T-shirt all day every day, life would be so much better. Why can't I live somewhere like San Diego, where on cold days it's like 75 degrees.

"Patrick, wait up!"

"I stop and turn, squinting through the crowd. Elliot's weaving toward me, his smile like it's been waiting all day to break through the noise.

"What are you doing after school? Scratch that—I know. You're going home to sulk in your dungeon and pretend people don't exist."

"Not true," I lie.

"Come on," he says, already walking. "Annie's. First-day milkshake tradition. It's happening."

I want to say no. I should say no. But something in me is too tired to argue.

Maybe it's not about the milkshake.

Maybe it's just that I don't want to be alone tonight.

"I don't know; Mom wants me home."

"Your mom doesn't care what you do, don't lie to me. I'm your best friend, let's go to Annie's." He insists.

"Okay, I guess." I finally cave. After all, I do really like the milkshakes at Annie's. Jessi and I would always go there during the summer, on days when she didn't have cheer, STUCO. or another extra-curricular activity that was requisite for her to attend.

When we get to the diner, I can tell a lot of the students had the same idea. The parking lot is packed Elliot and I circle the parking lot in his car looking for a spot. We find one on our second trip around and we begin debating if we are hungry or just want milkshakes.

We both decide on milkshakes and I can tell that Elliot is checking in, to see how I am really doing. I can see the wheels turning in his head as he tries to figure out which question to start with.

"How was your summer man?" Elliot asks, "I left with my grandparents on a cross-country trip and I spent the whole summer sightseeing with them.

"It was okay, just stayed home mostly." I don't give a long answer, because I really didn't do much. I played video games and stayed in my basement when I was home. I didn't leave often, because other than Elliot, I really don't have any friends.

I mostly just nod. But he's watching me.

He knows I'm holding something in.

"Did you go back to the farm this summer?" he asks.

I freeze for a second. Then nod. "Yeah."

"How was it?"

I stare at my milkshake, watching the whipped cream melt into the swirl.

"Hard," I say. "Hot. Quiet. A lot of work."

"Sounds about right."

"It was the first time I'd been up there without her."

He doesn't say anything. Doesn't need to. That's why he's Elliot.

"We used to spend every summer there," I add. "Baling hay, chasing goats, stealing popsicles from Grandma's freezer. Jessi hated the smell, but she always helped anyway. Said it was our thing."

I swallow hard. I can feel the tears building.

"This year... it felt empty. Like the whole place was holding its breath, waiting for her to come running out of the barn. Hair flowing behind her. Smile radiating. And she never did."

There's a long pause. I don't look up.

"I'm sorry, man," Elliot says quietly. "That's brutal."

I nod. That's all I can do. Sniffling in silence.

"You know you don't have to go through it alone, right?" he adds. "Like... I get it. I really do. I lost both of my parents when I was ten. And I hated everyone who told me it would get better. But it does. Slowly. Like... glacially slow. But it *does*."

"Yeah," I say. "I know."

We sip our shakes in silence for a minute, the kind that isn't awkward. The kind that feels like understanding.

"So," Elliot says, nudging me, "you think we'll survive this year?"

"Doubtful," I say. "But at least there's milkshakes."

We laugh, and for the first time in a long time, it doesn't feel forced.

Chapter 6 – The Weight of Normal

The milkshake was good. The laughter felt real. But the feeling didn't last. It never does.

Monday disappeared without warning. Then Tuesday—quiet, cold, and way too early.
Then Wednesday. Then Thursday. All blurring into a smear of bells, whispers, and forced smiles.

I move through the hallways like a ghost—there but not really.

Elliot keeps trying. He cracks jokes, walks with me between classes, even offers to study together. But I'm not ready. Not yet.

Every time I start to feel okay, guilt slips in and shuts it down. Like I'm not allowed to smile. Like I'm betraying her when I do.

In English, we're starting our narrative writing unit. Mrs. Carson paired us up, but I asked to work alone. She gave me that "I see more than you want me to" look but said yes.

The prompt is simple: write about a memory. Something real. Something personal.

I stare at the blank page, pen in hand.

All I can think about is Jessi. The passenger seat. Her voice. The sound of the radio just before everything changed.

But I don't write any of that down.

Not yet.

It's finally Friday.

Today is the one day of the week I look forward to—not because of football games, but because I get two whole days without crowded hallways, fake smiles, and people like David Bell. I suffer through each class completing the worksheets or the in-class assignments and trudge through my day. At 2:25 the bell rings and I am free for two whole days from this prison, they call school.

Freedom.

I push through the school doors, ready to disappear—

And there he is.

David Bell.

Standing with his usual crew of letterman jackets and overconfident grins. Aliza's beside him, arms folded, half-listening. They're mid-brag about tonight's game when they spot me.

Laughter. Pointing. Like clockwork.

All of them laugh—except Aliza. She smacks David's chest and says something sharp. I can't hear what. But it's enough to make him pause.

Then he heads straight for me.

He doesn't walk—he charges. And suddenly the crowd parts like they know a show's about to start.

My heart stutters. Fight or flight.

I don't move.

"Schwartz! What's going on, man?" David beams like we're old friends. His crowd snickers behind him.

"You coming to the game tonight? We're gonna *annihilate* the Tigers."

"Probably not," I say, voice low. "Not really my thing."

"Aw, come on." He pulls a folded ticket from his back pocket and waves it in my face. "I've got one just for you. Consider it a peace offering. New year, new page—right? We're seniors. Let's enjoy it."

He holds it out, firm. Too firm.

I hesitate. Waiting for the punchline. The setup. The *but.*

It doesn't come.

Everyone's watching. The ticket just hangs there like bait.

I take it. Slowly.

"There we go," David says, flashing a smile way too wide. "I'll look for you in the stands tonight."

The bus doors hiss open behind me.

"Don't be rude now, Schwartz," David calls as I step on. "Wouldn't want to waste a gift."

I drop into my seat and stare at the ticket in my hand. It's warm from his. Thin, glossy. Too light to carry the weight it does.

Is it real? A trick? A setup?

Why would David Bell—a walking ego in cleats—want me at his game?

I shove the ticket into my backpack without looking at it again.

Part of me wants to rip it up.

The other part... isn't sure why I haven't.

Chapter 7 – When the Lights Find You

"Patrick…. PATRICK, THIS YOUR STOP!" the bus driver yelled.

The bus driver's voice snaps me back to reality. She must've called my name a few times, because as I step off, the whispers have already started.

"What a loser…"
"He's so weird…"

They think I can't hear.

I always hear.

"Sorry, Ma'am I didn't hear you.. Thanks." I told the bus driver. I don't know her name, she has been my driver the last couple years, but I never talk to her. I think her name is Miriam or Maureen, something close to that. She has a son in my grade and one a couple years younger. We used to ride bikes together. That was back when things felt normal. Before life got stuck in rewind.

3:05 pm

I step through the front door and as expected mom is already halfway through a bottle of wine. I hear the slurred echo of Dr. Phil coming from the living room. She's shouting at the TV like she is personally offended.

She doesn't see it—that she's exactly like the ones she mocks.

My dad isn't home; he normally doesn't get home until about six. And when he does, the routine never changes: open a beer, drop into the recliner, and watch whatever game is on. Rockies if they're playing. Broncos if they're not. Doesn't matter if it's a rerun.

We used to go out to dinner sometimes.

Now it's microwave dinners and silence.

I clean up the kitchen—put away the bottle she left on the counter, toss the empty wine glass in the sink—and head downstairs.

As soon as I hit the bottom step, I call Elliot.

"I don't know, I just feel like the whole thing is a set up." I tell him pacing. "Nothing good can come from going to tonight's game. I think I am going to just stay in."

"Wrong answer," he says immediately, "You've gotta start somewhere, man. Baby steps. And this is one of them. I'm going. We'll go together. Kickoff is at 7, so I will pick you up around 6:30."

"I'm just not sure." I stammer

"You're going!" He doesn't give me a chance to respond, "I'll see you at 6:30. Don't make me drag you out."

The line goes dead.

I stare at my phone. I guess that's it.

I'm going.

5:30 pm

I shower and get dressed—something better than what I wore to school. If I'm showing up to a football game for the first time in two years, I might as well look halfway human.

I have time to kill, which almost makes me more nervous. I try not to think about it.

When Dad walks through the door, I'm already on the couch—just sitting there, watching the Reds and Rockies.

It's strange. I can't remember the last time I sat here next to him.

He drops into his chair, cracks open a can, and starts yelling at the TV.

Then something even stranger happens.

He glances over at me.

"Where the heck do you think you're going tonight?"

"I thought I'd catch the football game," I say.

He looks at me like I just told him I'm moving to Canada.

"Really?"

"Yeah. Just… figured I'd check it out."

The silence between us stretches longer than it should.

"Well… have fun. Enjoy the game."

I blink.

"Enjoy the game."

They're simple words. But they're the first thoughtful thing my dad's said to me in months. Maybe longer.

Before I can process it, a horn honks outside. Elliot. Right on time.

I grab my jacket and head for the door.

As I step out, I glance back.

This year might actually be manageable.

If I let it.

Chapter 8 – Flicker, Then Fade

6:50 pm

The stadium lights buzzed overhead like angry wasps.

I stood outside the fence for a full five minutes before I finally walked in.

Elliot waiting with unsure of my hesitation—but not pushing me, either.

I wasn't wearing school colors. I didn't own any.

When we finally made it through the gates, Elliot headed straight for the student section. I followed a few steps behind.

The second we reached the bleachers, it was like stepping into another world.

Everyone lit up when they saw Elliot—shouting his name, high-fiving him, pulling him into conversations. He's always been that guy: funny, good-looking, impossible not to like.

Then they saw me.

And everything changed.

The laughter died down. The smiles faltered.

Some people gave a quick, awkward hello. Others looked right through me, like they do in the halls. Like I'm still the ghost everyone's too afraid to talk to.

No one was mean. Just... quiet.

And honestly, that silence felt louder than anything else in the stadium.

The three hours of "watching" football went by faster than I expected.

It was less about the game and more about talking with Elliot—about anything and everything except what either of us was actually thinking.

Of course, David was right—we crushed the other team.

"It's always good to get the first W under your belt," my dad would say.

Although, if his team loses, it's a bad day for everyone.

After every home game, there's a post-game hangout called the 5th Quarter—hosted by one of the churches. It's meant to keep kids out of trouble: pizza, video games, flirting in the corner until two in the morning.

Elliot asks if I want to go.

"No, I think I'm just going to head home. It's a little after 10 and I've had a long day. Thanks though."

"Are you sure, it's never as fun going alone, as it is going with someone you know." Elliot pleads.

"Come on," he says. "Could be fun. You might even make a friend."

I roll my eyes. "No, I'm good. It's already past ten and I've used up all my social energy for the month."

He laughs. "You're sure? It's not the same going alone."

"I'm sure," I say. "Maybe next week."

He nods and offers to drop me off before heading over.

I walk in the house still laughing at something dumb Elliot said. My dad glances up from the game, surprised—maybe because I'm smiling.

"Night," I say.

He nods. "Glad you went."

Down in the basement, I sit on my bed and let the silence settle.

Was that happiness?

A real laugh. A real smile. A real moment that didn't hurt.

David gave me a ticket. Elliot took me. Some classmates even said hi.

For once, it all felt... okay.

Too okay.

Like the kind of moment you don't realize is the top of the hill—until you start falling.

I didn't know it then.
But everything was about to come crashing down.
And I wasn't ready.

Blake Collins

Chapter 9 – Echoes of the Unseen

That night, I fall asleep faster than I have in months.

No tossing. No pacing. No staring at the ceiling wondering if I'll ever feel okay.

Just sleep.

And then—

The world goes dark again. Suddenly, I'm wet.

Soaked through. Lying on my back.

Flashing red lights spin across the sky. The pavement is cold beneath me. It's dark. My head is pounding.

I try to sit up, but three men press me down. I don't recognize them. Their hands are heavy and urgent.

"Don't move," one says. "You're okay. Just lie still."

Another voice, louder, more persistent: "What's your name? Can you tell us your name?"

I want to answer, but I can't think. My head is splitting. Everything is spinning.

Then it hits me.

The accident.

"Patrick," I whisper. "My name's Patrick."

I fight through the pain, searching the darkness with my eyes.

"Where's Jessi? Where's my sister?"

No one answers.

The world fades.

I wake up in a hospital bed.

My mouth is dry. My chest hurts. Jessi is nowhere.

"Where is she?" I ask the empty room. "Where is my sister?"

Panic takes over. I try to sit up, but my arms are weak.

Then the door bursts open.

Mom rushes in first, eyes red, cheeks wet.

Dad follows—slower, quieter.

I can tell he's worried. He's just not the type to show it unless the Rockies are blowing a 9th inning lead.

And that hug—maybe the last time my mom truly held me like she meant it.

I close my eyes, seeking solace, and a memory surfaces:

Jessi and I, sitting on the back porch, sharing a bowl of popcorn, our laughter echoing into the night sky as we watched fireflies dance.

Her smile, so radiant, so full of life.

That moment, so simple, yet so profound.

It seems like a lifetime ago.

Those memories.

But in my dreams, it still feels like I'm bleeding.

I woke up with that memory still in my head—Jessi laughing under the stars.

But the ache in my chest reminded me it was just a dream.

Still, I held onto it for as long as I could.

Because somehow, even after the nightmare, life went on.

Chapter 10 – The Quiet Tally

The weeks that followed were strangely quiet.

September faded into October, and things at school started to feel almost... routine. I went to class, left class, and survived the day with as little attention as possible.

Occasionally, I'd join Elliot at a football game, just to prove I still existed. And oddly enough, people started to notice. Some even said hi.

It was small, but it was something.

Homecoming was two weeks away. Normally, I would've scoffed at the idea—too loud, too fake, too many people pretending they cared about things that didn't matter.

But this year felt different.

Even David Bell had been... oddly civil. Saying "what's up" in the hallway. Smiling like he wasn't the same guy who used to shove me into lockers.

I didn't trust it.

But I noticed it.

Maybe the whole year had felt seamless so far.

Too seamless.

We were sitting in fifth period, just after lunch, when Principal Powell's voice crackled over the intercom.

"Boys and girls, during this period your teachers will now be passing out the ballots for Homecoming King and Queen."

I tuned out the rest. It didn't matter. Everyone knew it'd be David and Aliza. They were seniors, captains of everything, and the golden couple of Black Hills High. Voting just made it look fair.

Señor DeLeon walked down the aisle passing out the ballots.

"Recuerden… todos tienen una voz que necesita ser escuchada," he said, smiling.
"Everyone has a voice that needs to be heard."

I took mine, expecting to check boxes I didn't care about and toss it in.

David Bell was right there at the top. No surprise.

Under "Queen," another cheerleader. Then, second on the list—Aliza Gillespie. Of course.

I glanced down the page.

There were five names for each list.

And then—I froze.

Number five.

Patrick Schwartz.

I stared at it like it was a typo. I kept waiting for the ink to smear or the letters to rearrange—anything to prove it wasn't real. It wasn't my name in that spot.

I looked again.

Still there.

I checked the box next to David's name—because I didn't want this—and turned it in without saying a word.

I saw Elliot in the hallway. He was grinning like a maniac.

"Dude! You made the ballot! The actual ballot!"

"Yeah," I said, like it was no big deal. Like my head wasn't still spinning. But things like this don't just happen to people like me—not without a reason.

"This is huge. People are actually talking about it—like, the whole school."

"It's not like I want to win," I muttered. "I probably won't even go to the dance."

"You might have a shot," he said. "Almost everyone in my fifth period said they were voting for you."

"They did not."

"Swear."

"Why would anyone vote for me?" I asked, half-laughing. "It's gonna be David and Aliza. Just like always. They basically own this place."

Elliot shrugged. "Still cool, though."

We headed to class, both of us still laughing. But somewhere deep in my chest, something wasn't sitting right.

What were the odds?
Me—of all people.
Was this real? Or was I the punchline in a joke I didn't get yet?

I shrugged it off, like always, and finished out the day trying to be invisible.

Only now, I wasn't.

People started looking at me in the halls. Saying hi. Smiling.

Like I'd suddenly become someone worth noticing.

And that's what scared me the most.

Because if Jessi were here, she'd probably laugh. Tell me I deserved it. Say something sarcastic like, 'Took them long enough.'

But she's not here.

And all I can do is wonder what she'd think of the version of me that's left.

Chapter 11 – The Weight of Their Gaze

It's Friday.

Homecoming.

Nothing much has changed—except the buzz.

The halls hum with whispered predictions, wide-eyed guesses, and fake suspense over something everyone already knows.

> Mr. and Ms. Perfect are going to win. They always do.

I just want to get the day over with.

When the intercom crackles to life, I already know what's coming.

"Hello, Principal Powell here," he says, voice as cheery and flat as ever. "As you all know, there will be a game this evening between the Bulldogs and the Phantoms. This is Homecoming, so we will honor the court at midfield during halftime."

He goes on to name each class representative, starting with the freshmen.

I tune it out.

I've checked out of senior year already—and it's only October.

Same faces. Same fake laughs. Same teachers pretending they know me.

I stare out the window, counting the minutes until 2:25.

"Finally," Powell says, "for the senior court, your Homecoming Queen is... Aliza Gillespie."

The hallway erupts—cheering, clapping, laughter.

No surprise.

Then—

"And your Homecoming King is..."

I mouth the name like a reflex. *David Bell.*

"Patrick Schwartz."

Silence.

Not just in the classroom. The whole hallway goes still.

I feel every set of eyes turn in my direction.

I stare at the speaker in the corner next to the American Flag.

Like maybe it's broken.

Like maybe it glitched.

But it didn't.

"Go Phantoms," Powell says with forced excitement.

The bell rings. 2:25.

But no one moves.

2:25

My jaw might've bounced off the table.

Never in a million years did I want this. I didn't expect it.

Heck, I don't even like half the people who supposedly voted me in.

I kept waiting for someone to yell 'just kidding'—like one of those TikToks where they prank the kid at prom with a fake nomination. But nothing.

Just silence.

Then movement.

I grabbed my stuff and stepped into the hallway.

And just like that, *every* set of eyes locked on me.

Like I'd grown wings. Or caught fire. Or both.

Mrs. Carson stepped out of her room as I passed and pulled me into a hug.

I let her. I've had teachers hug me before. It's not my thing—but hers felt... different.

"I am so proud of you, Patrick!" she said, beaming. "Why didn't you tell me you were on the ballot? Or that you even wanted this?"

"Honestly?" I said. "I was shocked when I saw my name. And I didn't think I had a chance. I didn't even want it."

"Well, after everything you went through last year," she said, eyes softening, "if anyone deserves this, it's you. I mean that. I'm proud of you."

I felt my face heat up. "Thanks."

I slipped away down the hall, ready to be done with school for the day—

—but then I ran straight into David Bell.

"Schwartz," he said, his voice low and sharp, "you and I need to talk."

His tone stopped me cold. He wasn't shouting, but something about it made my stomach twist.

"Okay… about what?"

"I just want to congratulate you," he said, but his smile didn't reach his eyes. "I always thought it'd be her and me senior year. But hey—congrats."

"I didn't think I'd win," I said. "I still don't get it."

"Neither do I."

There was a beat of silence.

Then he clapped me on the back—too hard.

"You got a date for the dance?"

"Uh… not yet."

"Well, better find one quick. Nothing like last minute, huh?" He laughed.

"We'll all see you tonight," he said as he walked away. "All eyes on you."

Then he paused, turned slightly, and added,

"Everyone's gonna remember this weekend forever."

He grinned.

Then he disappeared into the crowd.

I stood there, frozen.

What did that mean?

I hustled home, still trying to unpack his words.

"Everyone's gonna remember this weekend."

It echoed in my head. Over and over.

I found a clean-ish pair of jeans, a black button-up shirt, and a blue tie that matched our school colors—buried in the back of my dad's closet.

My dress shoes hadn't seen the light of day since the funeral. They were a little small, but they would have to do. I didn't have the time to go pick out a new wardrobe.

I called Elliot and asked him to pick me up by five. I had to be back at the school for pictures with Aliza before the game.

Mom was planted on the couch, halfway through a bottle, yelling at Dr. Phil in her afternoon ritual.

Dad wouldn't be home until late.

Neither of them had been to a game since Jessi.

I didn't even bother telling them I was being honored at halftime.

5:00

Elliot showed up right on time.

I was ready. Or as ready as I could be.

Already soaked in sweat—and I hadn't even stepped outside yet.

I might as well have jogged to the high school in the 70-degree weather. My shirt clung to my back like I'd just sprinted a mile.

Elliot didn't even bother ringing the doorbell. He just walked right in and came straight downstairs.

"Dude," he said, bursting into laughter, "Did you shower with your clothes on?"

"Shut up, Elliot. I'm nervous." I sniffed my armpits. "Do I smell?"

"Please don't do that on the field. Or near Aliza," he said, still laughing.

"I'm serious," I snapped. "I need help, man. I don't know how to do any of this."

Elliot raised his hands in surrender. "Alright, alright. All joking aside—you look good. You don't stink. You're just nervous, and that's normal."

He looked at me, more serious now.

"You always think the worst is gonna happen. But it won't. This is gonna be fine. Just like it's fine for every other guy who's stood out there. You deserve this."

I nodded, trying to believe him.

"Come on," he said. "If we don't leave now, you'll be late."

We ran upstairs.

Mom didn't even glance up from the couch. Dr. Phil was still preaching and the wine glass was still full.

I could've been on fire and she wouldn't have noticed—unless I blocked the TV.

Chapter 12 – The Jester and the Queen

5:55 p.m.

We pull up to the high school just in time.

Everyone on the court is filing in, most of them with their parents.

For a second, I feel it—that tiny ache in my chest. I wish mine were here. Even just one of them.

But then I glance at Elliot—grinning like a kid in a candy store—and maybe I'm the lucky one.

Maybe they should be envious of me.

As we walk inside, the first person I see is Aliza.

And she is... stunning.

Long black hair, sun-kissed skin, and a royal blue dress that makes her look like something out of a storybook. Not just beautiful—**regal**. Like a real-life queen.

Her parents are snapping photos from every angle while she politely poses, but she looks like she's over it. Tired, maybe. Waiting.

"Patrick! You made it! I've been waiting for you!"

She doesn't even wait for the next picture. She walks straight over and pulls me into a hug.

"You clean up well," she says, smiling.

I smile back, trying to act normal, even though my brain short-circuits the second I catch her scent—sweet, like bubblegum or cotton candy. Subtle. Hypnotizing.

After the hug, she turns to her parents.

"Mom, Dad—this is Patrick. He's the Homecoming King."

Then, like it's the most natural thing in the world:

"He's a super nice guy. Honestly, the students couldn't have picked a better person."

Her parents beam.

They're warm, easy to talk to. I was nervous for nothing.

It kind of feels like meeting a girlfriend's parents, even though I've never actually had that experience.

There's pressure in moments like this—not just to impress, but to not ruin her night.

Our night.

We take a few pictures together—her arm around my back, my arm around her waist—and for a moment, we look like something real.

Then *David Bell* walks in.

And it's like a switch flips.

The flashes stop. The attention shifts.

One second, I'm next to her. The next, I'm background noise.

"David, it's so good to see you! Oh my, how handsome—you always clean up so well," Aliza's mom says.

"Thanks, Mrs. Gillespie," David replies smoothly. "But enough about me—your daughter looks radiant."

His voice is different. Polished. Respectful.

I've never heard him sound like that before.

This is the David the teachers love. The one who knows how to play a room full of adults.

With students, though? He's someone else entirely.

"Patrick!" he says, turning to me like he just remembered I existed. "Didn't even recognize you. You look great, man. You ready for tonight?"

"Yeah, I think so—ready or—"

He's already moved on.

Talking to Aliza's dad like I was never there.

Typical.

As David launched into full politician mode with Aliza's dad, I took a step back. Just enough to give them space. Just enough to be forgotten again.

The laughter between them rose, smooth and practiced.

I stared down at the gym floor, my shoes suddenly too shiny, my tie too tight.

"Hey."

The voice was quiet, but unmistakable.

I looked up. Mrs. Carson.

She stood just off to the side, holding a clipboard, like she was helping organize the court's lineup or supervising the photos.

Her eyes softened when they landed on me.

"I saw you come in," she said gently. "I just wanted to say—seeing you here tonight? You're doing more than you know."

I opened my mouth, unsure of what to say. But she wasn't expecting a reply.

"You've got a lot of people in your corner, Patrick. Whether you realize it or not."

She gave me a small nod and moved back toward the check-in table, clipboard in hand like it was nothing. Like she hadn't just handed me a lifeline.

And for a moment, I didn't feel so invisible.

6:45 p.m.

We head toward the stadium and meet under the bleachers. A crowd has already formed, buzzing with nervous excitement.

"I want everyone on their best behavior," Principal Powell announces. "This is a special night—not just for you, but for your families, the seniors on the field. No shenanigans. Do you understand?"

"Yes," we all reply in unison.

We pair up, arms locked, two-by-two. Aliza and I are last—senior royalty, marching behind everyone else. We wait near the corner of the end zone.

With every couple that walks across the field, a confetti cannon fires—blue and black exploding skyward. Only one set is working, but no one seems to mind. It still looks magical.

"You ready?" Aliza asks.

"Yeah," I say, my voice shaky. "Just nervous."

"Don't be. It'll be over in five minutes. I've got you."

She smiles.

And for a second, I believe her.

There's a calm in her voice, in the way she looks at me—like nothing bad can touch us, at least not right now.

It reminds me of Jessi.

The way she'd grab my hand before something scary. Tell me to breathe. Promise I'd be okay.

I haven't felt that kind of warmth since the accident.

And tonight, for just a second, I let myself feel it again.

"And I'm sorry about David," she adds. "He's been so cruel. I've told him to stop, but he doesn't listen. I just... I want you to know—I like you. I really do."

Her voice is soft, but sincere.

And in that moment, I didn't feel alone.

Before I can even reply, they call our names.

We begin the walk.

As we step into the spotlight, the crowd erupts—cheers, applause, flashes.

Most of it's for Aliza, but I hear my name a few times.

I catch Elliot in the front row of the student section—grinning and waving like I was a celebrity and he was my biggest fan.

For the first time in... forever, I feel seen.

I feel *okay*.

We reach the fifty-yard line and turn to face the home side. The crowd is loud, the lights are bright, and everything is spinning in the most perfect way.

The cannons fire.

Confetti rains down—blue and black, swirling in the wind.

I'm smiling. She's smiling.

Then—another pop.

Louder. Closer.

The crowd gasps.

And suddenly, I'm drenched.

Not in confetti.

In paint.

Bright pink paint.

It hits like a wave—thick, sticky, and cold. Aliza screams beside me.

The cheer dies.

The laughter starts.

Not all at once—just murmurs at first. Snickers. A few chuckles from the student section. A whoop from one of the football players.

Aliza runs, tears streaking her cheeks, paint in her hair.

And I'm left standing alone, soaking in shame.

I am not a king.

I never was.

I'm the jester.

The joke.

The punchline.

My legs move on their own—off the field, toward the tunnel. Away from the stares, the silence, the smirks.

By the time I reach the exit gate, I hear footsteps behind me.

It's Elliot.

I hate this," he says, voice cracking. "You were finally happy. Just for one night. And they couldn't even let you have that."

"I *told* you," I snap, spinning to face him. My voice breaks. "You made me come. This is your fault."

He flinches.

But I don't stop.

"Why don't you just do what everyone else does and pretend I don't exist?"

He opens his mouth, but I don't let him speak.

"I'm so sick of people pretending they care," I snap. My voice is breaking. "It's all fake. All of it."

My fists are shaking. My throat's tight.

"I never should've come. I should've known better."

I shove past him, storming toward the parking lot.

He doesn't follow.

I regret every word the second it leaves my mouth.

But I don't turn around.

I can't.

I'm too angry.
Too hurt.
Too hollow to face what I've said.

I just told off the one person who never gave up on me.

And for what?

Out of seven billion people on this planet…

I've managed to push away the only one still willing to call me a friend.

Chapter 13 – Utterly and Completely Alone

For the second time in my life, I feel truly, inescapably alone.

No Jessi.
No Elliot.
No parents.
No one.

Just silence.

The kind that swallows you whole.

I sit in the dim light of the basement—my own personal cave carved from grief. The air feels heavier down here tonight, like even it's given up trying to comfort me. The soft glow of my Xbox pulsing in standby mode is the only light in the room. It hums faintly from the corner, waiting—like it always is. A mindless escape I can't even bring myself to touch.

I used to think I had at least one person left. Elliot. My best friend since kindergarten. The only one who stood by me when everyone else turned their backs.

And now he's gone too—because I shoved him away.

Not because he deserved it.
Not because he did anything wrong.
Because I was angry. Humiliated. Drenched in paint and shame and fury.
And he was there.

That's it. That's the reason.

He was *there*.

Aliza was there too—collateral damage in a war she didn't sign up for. She trusted David, and he used her. Just like he used me. Just like he's always done.

I should've protected her.

Instead, she got hit by the same blast meant for me.

The phone rings.

I ignore it.

It rings again. And again. The sound feels like a mosquito buzzing inside my skull.

Fourth call.

I answer—not because I want to, but because maybe part of me still hopes someone cares.

"What do you want?" I snap. "Can't you just let me be? I've been humiliated enough."

There's a pause.

Then a quiet, tearful voice:
"Patrick… it's me."

My heart stumbles.

Aliza.

She's crying. I can hear it in her breath—soft, shaky sobs trying to hold themselves together.

"I just… I wanted to say I'm sorry," she whispers. "I haven't even told David yet, but I'm breaking up with him tonight. I can't do it anymore. He doesn't care who he hurts—he just wants to be the center of attention. And tonight… he got what he wanted. At our expense."

Her voice cracks.

"I meant what I said earlier. I care about you, Patrick. You're kind. You're real. And you didn't deserve what happened."

I close my eyes, jaw tight, trying to will back the tears threatening to spill.

"I'm sorry for everything," she says. "I hope… I hope your night gets better. Goodnight."

The line goes dead.

And I'm alone again.

Alone with the echo of a voice that was kind, and the silence that followed.

What now?

Do I call her tomorrow? Do I show up to the dance, pretending I didn't just get torn apart in front of the entire school? Do I face them—David, the football team, the whispers, the laughter?

Do I even go back to school?

Twenty minutes ago, I wasn't sure I'd survive senior year.

Now I'm wondering if I'll survive the night.

I stare at my phone for a long time.
I scroll to Elliot's name.

I want to call him. I want to say I'm sorry. That I didn't mean it. That I lashed out because I had nothing left to give and nowhere left to place the pain.

But I remember the look on his face.
The way he flinched when I told him to pretend I didn't exist.
The way he stood there—hurt, stunned, trying to help—while I burned the last bridge I had left.

He didn't deserve that.
No one deserves to be thrown away like that.

Especially not someone who's been pulling you out of the fire your whole life.

But that's what I do, isn't it?

Push people away before they leave me.

Now I'm left with the aftermath.
The cold.
The silence.
The overwhelming weight of knowing this is all my fault.

Not just tonight. Not just the paint, or the shouting, or the broken friendships.
All of it.

If I had been paying attention…
If I hadn't looked away for half a second…
If I had *done something differently*, even the smallest thing—maybe she'd still be here.

I was supposed to be her protector.

I replay it all the time.
That final moment. The sound. The silence that followed.
The way I felt in the hospital bed, asking for her before anyone had the heart to answer.

People say it wasn't my fault.
They say "accidents happen."
But the truth is, no matter how many times someone says it out loud…
I don't believe them.
Not really.

Because no matter how much I want to forget…
I remember.

Every.
Single.
Night.

I lie back on my bed, staring at the ceiling. My thoughts swirl like a storm I can't escape.

Aliza's paint-covered face.
Elliot's heartbroken eyes.
The crowd's laughter.
David's smug grin.

And then I hear it again. Not in the hallway this time, not even in a dream—just in my head, as sharp as ever:
"Nice look, Phantom King. Guess you finally found your crown."

I clench my fists. There's no one here. No one laughing in the shadows. Just me, trapped with a voice I can't shut off.
That's the worst part. David doesn't even have to be near me anymore—he lives in my skull, replaying every humiliation on a loop.

Jessi's voice follows, softer, like a ghost I can't let go of.

I know what's coming.
The dream.

It always comes when I feel like this—cornered, broken, raw. It waits until I'm too tired to fight back. Too numb to scream.

I try to stay awake. I beg myself not to close my eyes.

But the monster is already here.

It crawls into my chest, coils around my heart, and whispers all the things I'm terrified to believe.

This is who you are now.
This is all you'll ever be.
You don't deserve to be happy.
You killed her.

And deep down, I start to believe it again.

Because in this moment—this horrible, hollow moment—

I do not feel like a person worth saving.

Chapter 14 – The Path That Waits

I'm back in the hospital.

The smell of antiseptic burns in my nose. Machines beep in a rhythm I can't control. Tubes snake from my arms. My head aches. My chest feels hollow.

Outside the window, it's night. Or maybe it's just the way the room looks—dim, washed in blue.

I see them.

My mom and dad.

Pacing the hallway, their movements sharp and frantic like they've had this argument before. My mom's voice is muffled through the glass, but I can see her face. She's crying.

Then she looks in and sees me watching.

Her expression shifts. Pain overtakes panic. She walks into the room slowly, like she's afraid the truth might break me worse than the crash did.

"Where's Jessi?" I ask, sitting up too fast. Wires pull at my skin.

"Where is my sister? Why won't anyone answer me?"

My voice is shaking.

"You and Jessi were in a pretty bad accident," she says softly, brushing hair from my forehead. "You have some serious cuts and bruises. But you're going to be okay."

She pauses. Too long.

"What about Jessi?" I press. "Why aren't you with her? Is she even in the hospital? Is she okay?"

She looks away.

"Patrick…" Her voice breaks. "Your sister didn't make it."

Those words hang in the air like smoke. They don't settle. They don't make sense.

Didn't make it?

Didn't make it to the hospital?

Didn't make it out of surgery?

Didn't make what?

I blink, confused, the room spinning like I've lost gravity.

"What do you mean?" I whisper. "What do you mean?" I ask again, louder this time.

No answer.

I yank the IV from my arm. Blood streaks down my wrist. I tear off the monitors and stumble out of bed. I'm running now—down the hallway, past doors, past nurses who don't see me. The hospital walls stretch longer and darker with every step.

Suddenly, it changes.

The white halls fade into gray fog and forest. Trees twist out of the earth like claws. The floor beneath me is no longer tile, but damp soil and pine needles. The wind howls through the branches.

It starts to rain.

I don't know where I am, but I can't stop moving. I sprint through the trees, heart pounding, feet slick with mud. My hospital gown clings to my skin. Thunder cracks above me.

Then the path forks.

In front of me stands a crooked wooden sign. The words are carved into rotted planks:

Open your Eyes

Close your Heart

I freeze. My breath comes in gasps. I look down both paths, but neither reveals what's waiting. Just shadows. Darkness. More storms.

I don't choose.

I spin around and run the opposite way—but after a few minutes, I reach the same sign.

The same fork.

The same decision.

"What does this mean?!" I yell, but it comes out more like a plea. My voice cracks, swallowed by the trees.
"Open my eyes to *what*?"
"Close my heart to *who*?"
"I don't have anything left to close…"
"I've already lost everything."

The trees shudder around me like they've heard it all before.

The rain falls harder now—sharp and cold, like the sky is trying to cut me open.

Then… I feel it.

A presence.

From the shadows, something begins to emerge—tall, impossibly tall. Faceless. Cloaked in black, hood drawn low, the figure glides forward like a wraith stitched from smoke and silence. Its form bends the darkness around it, swallowing sound.

It doesn't speak at first.

It just *stares*—or at least, it feels like it. I can't see a face. But I can feel its eyes.

Watching.

Peeling me open.

"You know what this is," it finally says. The voice rumbles low, like thunder dragging across gravel.

"You know exactly what happened, Patrick."

I step back. "I don't. I don't know anything. I didn't mean to—I didn't—"

"You chose."

"No."

"You always had a choice."

"I didn't know—"

"And you *still* don't want to see it."

Its hand reaches out—long, bony fingers stretching toward my shoulder. They don't touch me at first. They just hover there, like the air itself is waiting to collapse.

Then the weight hits.

Heavy.

Crushing.

I collapse to my knees, trembling under the pressure, like the gravity around me has tripled. I can't breathe. My ribs won't expand. My body won't move.

I try to scream.

Nothing comes out.

I try to run.

My legs won't listen.

The figure leans down—its hood inches from my face. I can't see its eyes, but I *feel* them burrowing into mine. Burning. Peeling back everything I've hidden.

"You cannot outrun what's already inside you," it whispers. "You cannot unlive what's been done."

Something inside me snaps.

"Then why her?" I scream, my throat tearing with the sound. "Why Jessi? Why not me?" My voice ricochets through the trees, raw and broken. "If you're fate—if you're God—if you're whatever cruel thing that decided she should die and I should live—then screw you! Do you hear me? Screw you!"

I hurl the words until my voice is shredded, until my chest feels like it might split apart. The storm answers with thunder, deafening, but I scream louder, daring it to drown me out. My body shakes with rage, fire boiling through my veins.

I slam my fists into the ground, mud splattering up my arms. "Take me instead! Take me!"

The figure bends low, its hood inches from my face. Silence presses in—thicker than the rain, heavier than my own breath.

When it finally speaks, the words cut colder than the storm.

"You cannot trade places. You cannot unlive what's been done."

The silence hangs, suffocating. My breath rattles in my chest. For a heartbeat, I almost believe it might end here—just me, the storm, and the weight of what I've lost.

And then—

It lunges.

Chapter 15 – Still Here

8:30 a.m.

I wake up sprawled across my bed, my throat dry, my heart pounding like it's still stuck in that dream.
For a second, I don't even know where I am.
The shadows. The forest. The voice. The sign.
That figure. The weight of its hand. The way it said my name like it already knew everything I hated about myself.

Then I see them—my paint-soaked clothes still crumpled on the floor.

And it all rushes back.

Last night wasn't a dream.

The football field.
The laughter.

The Spotlight.
The phone call.
The figure in the woods wasn't real, but the humiliation? The loneliness? The truth?

That part never ended.

It all happened. And the only part I *imagined* was the moment I thought I could belong.

The last thing I clearly remember before surrendering to sleep's cruel mercy was hearing Aliza's voice on the phone. Soft. Shaken. Sincere.

She didn't have to call me. She didn't owe me anything. But she did.

And now questions swarm my brain like hornets in a jar.

Am I going to the dance tonight?
Is she expecting me to?
Would she still want to go with me—*after everything*?

Can I even walk back into that school… into that gym… after what they all saw?

After what they all *did*?

I sit up slowly. My body feels heavier than it should. Not sore. Just tired in a way that sleep can't fix.

All I know for sure is this: *Aliza reached out.* And that makes her the only person who still sees something in me.

But she's not my friend. Not yet. I don't know her well enough to call her that.

And right now—after the things I said to Elliot, after pushing away the one person who always stayed—I don't have *any* friends.

I'm alone.

Humiliated.

But maybe… I don't have to stay that way.

The water's hot, but it doesn't rinse off what's underneath.
The weight. The wreckage. The part of me still stuck on that field.

I dry off and open my closet. I pause, hand hovering over the usual black hoodie.

Then I spot something buried in the back. A shirt I haven't worn since before Jessi died.

It was her favorite.

She used to call it my "lucky shirt"—said the red made me look alive, like I actually belonged in the world. I remember her stealing it once and making me chase her through the house just to get it back. She wore it as a dress, laughing like she owned the place.

I haven't touched it since the accident.

But today, I pull it out and put it on.

Today needs to be different. Even if it hurts.

I barely recognize the person staring back.

Still broken. Still haunted.

But maybe not completely invisible.

I sit on the edge of my bed and grab a notebook from the nightstand. I flip it open and scribble a title at the top of the page:

Things I Need to Do Today:

Because if I'm going to stand up again… I need a plan.

I stare at the blank page for a long time.
The pen shakes a little in my hand.
It feels stupid, writing things down like this.
But maybe if I see it…
Maybe if it's real…
I won't fall apart again.

So I start.

Things I Need to Do Today:

1. *Make amends with Elliot.*

2. *Call Aliza.*

3. *Get a haircut.*

4. *Buy dress clothes.*

5. *Let myself be happy.*

I set the pen down and stare at the list.
It's not much.
But for the first time in a long time… it's something.

Chapter 16 – Red Means Go

10:00 a.m.

I decided to knock off the first item right away.

I head straight over to Elliot's house. At first, I run—but quickly realize I'm out of shape, so I slow to a walk. It takes me about ten minutes to make it to his front door. I knock, heart pounding like it's trying to crawl out of my chest.

His grandma answers.

Before I can say anything, she says, "I'm so sorry about what happened last night, Patrick. Whoever is at fault needs to be punished."

"Thanks," I say. "That means a lot. Is Elliot in? I really need to talk to him."

I glance past her and see him sitting at the kitchen table.

"He is. He said you were pretty upset last night and said some hurtful things." She hesitates, then softens. "Come on in. I'll make you some tea."

"Thank you," I say sincerely.

I step inside. It smells like mothballs and history—clean, warm, and old. There's a piano against the living room wall, polished like it's been waiting for someone to play it. The kitchen and living room are connected by an open archway. Elliot's sitting at the table, eating a bowl of cereal like it's any other day.

His grandma walks to the stove and sets the kettle on to boil.

"Hey, sorry about—" I start.

"Stop," Elliot cuts in. "It's not your fault. I know you were angry. I get it."

He looks me up and down. "Are you wearing... *color*? I think I need sunglasses to even look at you."

He laughs.

"It looks good," he adds. "Are you officially out of your 'black era'?"

"Shut up," I grin. "I'm trying something new… or old. I decided after last night, David Bell wasn't going to win. At least not easily. I'm done sulking around and being a victim. The old Patrick—the guy I used to be—starts today."

He gives me a once-over and smirks. "If that's true, then you need a haircut. You look like Samson or one of his concubines. You'd be pretty as a girl though."

I punch him in the arm. "I *know* it's on my list. Want to help me knock it out?"

"Do I have a choice?" he says, grinning. "Of course. I'll be your chauffeur."

The kettle whistles.

We sit down with warm lemon tea and cookies, chatting with his grandma and laughing about stupid memories from middle school. It's the first time in a long while I've felt… normal.

Afterward, I scratch off the first item on my list.

Make amends with Elliot.

"One down," I say aloud.

"What's next?" Elliot asks.

"I have to call Aliza."

I shift a little in my chair.

"She was the first person who reached out to me—other than you. She called last night. Apologized. Said she was breaking up with David… said she was tired of him hurting people just to get a laugh."

Elliot's jaw drops. "She called *you*? After all that?"

I nod.

"She said last night was the final straw."

We walk out onto the porch. Elliot is still trying to process it.

"Well, call her!" he says. "Wait—what are you even going to say?"

"I don't know yet. I was just going to ask if she's still going to the dance. I mean… it's senior year. They kind of expect the King and Queen to show up."

"You're *still* thinking about going?" he says, stunned. "Even after what happened last night?"

I shrug. "Honestly? I don't know. But I don't want to leave her hanging. She might not have a date. And if she wants to go... I don't want her to go alone."

Elliot nods slowly, then claps me on the back. "Well, call her. We've got stuff to do today."

I dial her number with shaky hands. It rings four times before going to voicemail. I hang up without leaving a message.

"No answer," I mumble. "She doesn't want to—"

My phone rings.

It's her.

Elliot nudges me. "Answer before she changes her mind!"

I fumble to swipe. "Uh, hello?"

"Hey," she says. Her voice is soft, tired. "I saw that you called."

"I was just wondering if you were still planning on going to the dance," I say. "If not, it's no big deal. I just didn't want to leave you out to dry."

"I broke up with David last night after he got home from the game. I called him and told him it was over."

I hear her breath catch, like she's holding back tears.

"I told him I wouldn't be going to the dance *with him*."

I jump in quickly. "That's okay, I get it—"

She interrupts me. "I didn't say I wasn't going. I said I wasn't going with *him*. Since neither of us have a date... maybe we could go with each other?"

She waits.

I freeze.

"Yeah," I finally say, blinking. "Yeah, that'd be great. I'll come to your house around five - thirty?"

"Perfect," she says. "It's a date. And by the way—my dress is red. You'll want to match."

She hangs up.

I just stare at the screen.

Elliot studies my face like I just told him I won the lottery.

"You okay?" he asks. "You're going? What did she say?!"

I hold up a hand. "Give me a second."

I explain everything. That it's real. That I'm actually going to the dance.

With *Aliza.*

Elliot's eyes go wide. "Dude. The captain of the cheer squad?"

I nod.

He laughs, then pauses.

"David's gonna kill you."

He's not wrong.

But I'm not afraid of David anymore.

We carried on with our list—one task at a time, checking things off like it meant something. And maybe, for the first time in a while, it did.

Next stop: dress clothes.

I went home with Elliot to ask my mom if she had any money I could use. When we got there, she was half-passed out on the couch, wine glass in hand, eyes glued to some overdramatic episode of *Dr. Phil.*

"Mom, can I have some money to buy clothes?" I asked.

She didn't look at me.

I tried again, louder this time. "Mom, *can I have some money*?"

"Yeah, sure. Purse is on the counter," she mumbled, not looking away from the TV.

I rifled through her bag, found a wad of cash, and we were out the door.

At the store, Elliot helped me pick out a pair of slacks, a crisp white dress shirt, and a red tie to match Aliza's new dress. Her original one had been ruined in the paint attack, and somehow that red tie felt symbolic—like maybe we were both choosing to wear color again.

I had shoes and a belt already. We were good to go.

Next item: haircut.

We pulled into the tiny barber shop on Main Street—the same one that's been there since I was a kid. The place hasn't changed in decades, down to the old cracked leather chairs and the bell on the door that chimes whenever someone walks in.

Henry, the town barber, was sitting behind the counter reading a paper. Bald, mid-70s, and known for saying whatever popped into his head, whether you wanted to hear it or not.

When I walked in, he squinted at me for a second, then smiled.

"Patrick," he said. "It's been a while. Sit down—I'll get you now."

He glanced at my hair and raised an eyebrow. "You're lookin' like one of them rockstars. Or a girl. Maybe both."

Classic Henry.

I sat down with Elliot to wait my turn. About two minutes later, he waved me over.

"What'll it be?" he asked, draping the cape over my shoulders.

"I'm not sure," I admitted. "Just… short. Like it used to be. Nothing too extreme. Just clean."

He nodded. "I got you."

Fifteen minutes later, I felt twenty pounds lighter. I looked down and saw a mountain of hair on the floor. Henry spun me around toward the mirror, and I almost didn't recognize myself.

It wasn't just the haircut. It was the way I looked at myself.

Like maybe—just maybe—I could be someone again.

"Thanks, Henry," I said, standing up. "I'll try not to be such a stranger."

He waved me off like he'd heard that before.

Elliot looked up from his magazine and busted out laughing. "Dude, you look amazing! Aliza's gonna freak out."

We'd spent most of the day getting things together. Afterward, Elliot dropped me off at my house so I could shower and get ready.

Chapter 17 – From the Ashes

I haven't been happy—*truly* happy—since Jessi.

The last item on my list wasn't something I could check off with a pen.
It was a reminder.
That to truly face David… and everything else I've been running from…
I need to let myself be happy.
I need to smile.

And tonight might be the first real chance I've had in a long time to do that.

I jump in the shower, towel off, and put on deodorant like it's any other night—but it isn't.
Not even close.

I slip into the new clothes: the crisp white dress shirt, the clean slacks, and the red tie.
My tie.
The one that matches Eliza's dress.

As I finish getting ready, my phone rings.

Elliot.

He says he's outside—with his date.

Her name's Erica. They've been friends for a while. Nothing serious, but enough to warrant a night out together. She's got this bubbly energy about her—always smiling, always saying what she's thinking. Blonde, captain of the soccer team, confident in a way I've never been.

I don't know her super well, but we've hung out here and there.

"I'll be right out," I say, then grab my phone, wallet, and jacket, and head out the door.

I hop into the back seat of Elliot's car, my heart already pounding.

We head straight to Aliza's.

Everyone knows where she lives.
But only the popular crowd ever actually *goes* there.

I never had.

She lives in the nicest part of town—a two-story brick house with a wrap-around porch and white columns that make it look like something out of a magazine. Her backyard stretches up toward the base of the mountains. You can see the ski resort from her street.

Her house is on the opposite side of town from mine. Twenty minutes away, but it feels like a different world entirely.

5:30 p.m.

We drove up Aliza's private drive, which felt like it stretched two miles long.
(It was probably only a quarter mile—but it *felt* longer.)

When we reached the front steps, the three of us walked to the door and waited.
It opened to reveal her mom—just as elegant and put-together as she was last night.

"Come in," she said warmly, stepping aside.

The entryway looked like something out of a movie. To the left was a grand spiral staircase—something you'd see in a castle. Straight ahead, the main living room opened up beneath twelve-foot ceilings. Two sleek couches framed a grand piano, and sunlight streamed in through towering windows.

This was, without a doubt, the nicest house I'd ever been in.

"I want to apologize again for what happened last night," Aliza's mom began, turning to me. "We never really liked David—just tolerated him, for Aliza's sake. I have to admit, though… he put on a good front. He almost had us fooled."

"It's really not a big deal," I lied.

"It was a *travesty,*" she said. "Aliza was devastated—she was up half the—"

"Mom, that's enough," Aliza interrupted gently.

The room fell quiet. All eyes turned toward her.

I cleared my throat. "I can understand that. It's actually because of your daughter that I'm here tonight."

I looked at Aliza, then back to her mom.

"I was angry. Bitter. Embarrassed. But then she called. She apologized—not that she had anything to apologize for. She was just as much a victim. But… she told me she cared." I paused, my voice breaking.

"And it hit me. That's when I realized I couldn't let David win. I couldn't keep hiding. I had to be the bigger person—and going to the dance tonight? That felt like the way to do it."

I glance over at Aliza, her eyes wet.

"I was stunned when she asked me to go with her. That's why I called. That's why I got my hair cut. I'm not just dressed differently tonight… I *feel* different. Closer to who I used to be. Closer to who I *want* to be.

The words spill out of me like they've been waiting for months. I don't even realize I'm crying until a tear rolls down my cheek.

I glance around the room. Elliot has tears in his eyes. Aliza too.

Then her mom walks straight over and wraps her arms around me.

reminds me of the hug Ms. Carson gave me in the hallway that day—the one where I thought I could hold it together, and then couldn't.
That moment where I realized someone still saw me… even when I didn't want to be seen.

This feels like that.

Maybe even stronger.

Like being pulled back from the edge by someone who doesn't even know how close you were to falling.

"I already like you better than David," she whispers in my ear, quiet enough that only I can hear.

I smile, eyes still blurry. "Sorry for the red eyes before pictures. Maybe we should get those out of the way so we can go enjoy senior homecoming. All of us."

They nod.

"Yes," everyone says at once, like it's obvious.

We gather together and take a few pictures, smiling through the remnants of emotion.
Then we pile into the car and head to dinner.

We piled into Elliot's car, all four of us still feeling the emotional weight from Aliza's living room—but no one said much about it. We didn't need to.

Some moments speak loud enough on their own.

Elliot drove, Erica in the passenger seat, while Aliza and I sat in the back. She kept glancing over at me with a soft smile, the kind that didn't need words to say, *I'm glad you're here.*

I didn't realize how tightly I'd been clenching my hands until I felt her reach over and gently squeeze one.

Not like a romantic gesture. Not yet.
Just… solid. Steady. Real.

As we drove across town, the sun was starting to dip below the mountains, casting long shadows across the road and tinting everything gold. It felt almost surreal—like time had slowed just for us.

Elliot broke the silence first.

"Okay, question for the car," he announced. "If you could only eat one food for the rest of your life, what would it be?"

"Easy," Erica said. "French fries. And ketchup doesn't count as a second food."

"Fries?" Elliot raised an eyebrow. "You'd die of salt."

"At least I'd die happy," she said, grinning.

We all laughed, and just like that, the mood started to shift. The car filled with small talk and random stories from school—teachers we liked, ridiculous rumors we'd heard, awkward dance moments from years past.

For the first time in forever, I wasn't thinking about Jessi, or David, or whether everyone at the dance would be staring at me.

I was just… *there.*

When we pulled into the restaurant, it was one of those cozy, low-light local places with warm lighting and worn wooden booths. Not fancy, but nice enough for a night like this.

We walked inside, the four of us still laughing about a story Elliot told where he accidentally wore two different shoes to school once and didn't notice until 4th period.

The hostess smiled and led us to a booth in the back.

Dinner was simple.
Good food. Easy conversation. Comfortable silences.

Aliza sat next to me, her shoulder brushing mine every now and then. I found myself leaning into her laugh—leaning into the way her eyes lit up when she talked about anything she cared about.

For the first time in a long time, I wasn't trying to escape the night. I was starting to *enjoy it.*

Chapter 18 – Glass Crowns

6:00 p.m.

After dinner, we head straight to the dance.

As we pull up, I spot limos and even a couple horse-drawn carriages lined up out front. Meanwhile, we're just parking in the student lot and walking in. And honestly? I don't even care.

When we step inside, we're instantly transported.

It's a *Winter Wonderland*—literally.
Ice sculptures glisten beneath soft blue lights. Balloons float like drifting snow. Blue and silver streamers hang from the ceiling like falling frost. The whole gym is unrecognizable. Magical.

Even before everything with Jessi… I wasn't really the "dance" type.
This is the *first* school dance I've ever attended.
And I'm in awe.

We agree to start the night by getting our pictures taken. The school's hired photographer has a little setup in the corner—lights, backdrop, the works.

Aliza and I pose like everyone else. She wraps her arms around my neck. I rest my hands on her waist. Classic.

But it's in that moment—up close, still—that I *really* see her.

Her dress.
The tight curls in her hair.
The red lipstick that matches her dress and makes her look… breathtaking.

She's stunning. Even more than yesterday. And yesterday, I didn't think that was possible.

And then I remember the last item on my list:
Let yourself be happy.

I smile.

Not the fake kind. Not the one I wear to convince people I'm okay.

It hits me—I'm not pretending. I'm not surviving. I'm just… happy. And that feels like a miracle.

After our pictures, we step aside and wait for Elliot and Erica to finish theirs.
The music's loud now—some upbeat song I don't recognize—and I lean in to catch what Aliza says.

Her lips are near my ear, my hand still resting at her waist.

"What?" I ask, leaning closer.

She repeats herself, right into my ear this time, warm and certain.

"Would you like to dance with me?"

I pause, a little stunned.

"I have to admit," I say, "I'm not much of a dancer… but I'd love for you to teach me. If there's anyone I'd want to dance with tonight, it's you."

She smiles and grabs my hand.

Without another word, she pulls me to the dance floor.

The opening notes of *Wonderwall* by Oasis drift through the speakers.
She pulls me into the same pose we used for our photo—arms around my neck, mine around her waist.

She looks up at me and starts mouthing the lyrics.

I get lost in her eyes.

In this moment.

In this feeling I didn't think I'd ever have again.

We spend the rest of the night laughing, dancing, talking with Elliot and Erica, and sharing quiet moments between songs. People we don't even know stop us to take pictures—friends of Aliza, kids from school who seem surprised to see *me* here, but somehow happy we are.

And through it all, she never leaves my side.

She's more than a date.

She's *present.*
Engaged.
Kind.

And I never feel alone.

With about an hour left in the dance, Principal Powell steps onto the stage, mic in hand.

The music fades. The lights dim.

"It's time to crown our Homecoming King and Queen," he announces.

"Would Patrick Schwartz and Aliza Gillespie please join me on stage?"

The spotlight hits us, and the room erupts into cheers and applause.
I glance at Aliza, stunned.

She grabs my hand, smiling.

We walk to the stage. I help her up the steps.

Principal Powell crowns her first—a silver tiara that sparkles like starlight under the gym lights.

Then he hands me a crown in school colors, along with a matching scepter.

We step forward, lights flashing, cameras snapping.

Her hand finds mine—fingers laced, not just held.
Not like friends. Not like a photo pose.
Like something more.

We take a few more pictures, and just before we turn to leave the stage, Aliza leans in and kisses me gently on the cheek.

And just like that, the crowd erupts again.

We head back across the dance floor, weaving through students who are cheering and calling our names.
Everyone's smiling. Even the people who never used to look twice at me.

We make our way back to Elliot and Erica. They're beaming.

We laugh, talk, and soak in the last few minutes of the night like it's all been scripted for us. For once, it feels like life is *letting up*.

Like maybe the worst is behind me.

As the dance winds down, we all agree—it's time to go.

The four of us walk out together, still buzzing from the night. Jokes fly back and forth, arms bumping, coats thrown over shoulders. It's the kind of moment that would've made Jessi smile.

"Tonight was perfect," I say, glancing at each of them. "Thank you all for everything. Really. Thank you."

And then I hear it.

Footsteps.

Heavy. Fast.

"PATRICK!"

I turn around just in time to see David Bell barreling toward me.

His face is red. Eyes wild.

"First, you steal my crown," he snarls. "Then, you steal my date. And now—now you're trying to steal my *girlfriend*?!"

I barely have time to register what he just said.

My mouth opens, but nothing comes out.

Then I see his fist coming.

Everything slows.

There's no time to move, to react, to defend.

The punch connects squarely with my jaw.

Pain explodes across my face, and the world tilts sideways.

Then everything goes black.

Chapter 19 – Open Your Eyes

I'm still falling.

An endless pit of black. No light. No ground.
It's like being swallowed whole—like that shadow from my dreams has finally won.
I'm losing hope. Drowning in something I can't fight.

I reach for anything—any branch, any rope, any hand—but there's nothing. Just the echo of my own voice: *Take me instead. Take me instead.*

The words bounce back at me, warped and hollow, until I can't tell if I'm screaming them or if they're screaming at me.

And then—silence.

A headstone rises from the dark. Jessi's name carved into it, glowing pale. I fall to my knees, clawing at the ground. "Trade me," I beg. "God, please—trade me. Let her come back. Take me instead."

But the headstone crumbles into dust. The earth splits open beneath me, and I'm swallowed whole.

I can't breathe. I can't fight. I can't wake up.

Until I do.

I jolt awake—sweating, panting.

But I'm not in my bed.

The room is unfamiliar. Soft lighting. Posters on the wall. A window cracked just enough to let in the early morning air.

Across the room, Elliot's slumped in a rocking chair, sound asleep.

I hear voices somewhere else in the house. Laughter, maybe. A soft clatter of dishes.

I sit up, and the movement stirs him.

"Hey, bud," Elliot says groggily. "How ya feeling? You took quite a fall last night."

He grins. "Hopefully you feel better than you look."

I rub my temples, trying to get my bearings. "I've got a splitting headache."
I pause, then look around. "Where are we?"

"Aliza's place," he says, stretching. "After David clocked you, she absolutely *lost it.* Started screaming at him, cursing him out, calling him every name in the book. Then, when he turned his back…" He pauses, laughing. "She sucker-punched him. Right between the eyes. Dropped him. It was beautiful."

"She didn't want to take you home. Said she wanted to keep an eye on you. She stayed with you most of the night."

Everything starts flooding back.
The dance.
The pictures.
Her hand in mine.
The kiss on the cheek.
Then… David calling my name.
Finally, the dream.

"Where is she now?" I ask.

"Your girlfriend?" he smirks. "She's downstairs."

We both laugh.

Then I go quiet.

Can I ask you something serious?" I say, my voice quieter than I expect.

Elliot straightens, like he already knows this isn't going to be light.

"How do you do it?" I ask. "How do you wake up every day and still… smile? Still laugh? After everything you've lost? Your parents… your life before. Most people wouldn't have survived half of what you've been through, and you're still—*you*. Kind. Whole. *Happy*."

He doesn't answer right away.

The silence stretches between us, full of everything he's never said out loud.

Finally, he breathes in slow and says, "Because I had to."

He looks me in the eye.

"If I didn't find something to hold onto… I would've drowned in it. The grief. The questions. The rage. I couldn't carry it all alone. So I didn't. I let people in. I trusted my friends. I leaned on them when I couldn't stand on my own. And slowly—*slowly*—I chose to start living again."

He pauses, then adds, softer now, "And honestly? A lot of that is because of you."

My throat tightens.

I look down, trying to swallow the lump in my chest. "Why can't things ever just... stay good for me?" I whisper. "Every time something starts to feel okay—normal—like I might be *okay* again… it crashes. Hard. The paint cannons. Getting knocked out. Jessi…"

I stop.

He doesn't rush in with a joke. He doesn't deflect.

Instead, he says, "I know it feels that way. Like you're cursed. Like you're meant to break."

His voice is steady, but there's something thick behind it—like maybe he's been there too.

"But look at what you *do* have, Pat. You've got a best friend who would walk through fire for you. A girl who looks at you like you're worth something—maybe more than either of you are ready to admit. And you? You've got this heart, man. This *huge*, hidden heart that you keep burying because you're scared of what happens when you let people see it."

He looks at me and finishes, "But people will love you. Just like I do. If you let them in… they'll stay."

nod slowly, then say, "I just wish I could remember everything from the night of the accident. I feel like it would explain why I feel like this all the time."

"Is it that you *can't* remember?" he asks. "Or that you *don't want* to?"

I hesitate. "I'm honestly not sure."

"Then that's what you need to figure out first. If you don't want to remember, that's okay. But it means you're still hiding from it. And if you really *can't*… well, maybe that's something you learn to live with."

I think about my dream.
The sign.

Open your eyes. Close your heart.

That sign from my dream comes back to me in full clarity now.

Maybe Elliot's right.

Maybe I've been choosing the second one all along.

Before I can say anything else, the door creaks open and Aliza steps in.

We fall silent for a second—caught in the weight of what was just said—but she doesn't seem to notice.

She grins.

"Good morning. How are you feeling?" she asks. "Your right eye looks pretty rough. Other than that, you look… decent enough."

"What were you two talking about?" she adds, walking toward us.

I hesitate, then smirk. "Last night. You know—Floyd Mayweather."

Elliot and I both laugh.

She narrows her eyes playfully. "Still got your sense of humor, huh? David didn't knock that out of you. Thank goodness. You're welcome, by the way. I did knock out a high school Quarterback for *you.*"

"Oh, I remember," I say, chuckling. "Thank you. I can't wait to see his face on Monday—especially when everyone finds out *you* did it."

"Stay on her good side," Elliot adds. "She's got a mean right hook. There was blood. Crying. It wasn't pretty."

"Not sure if it was David crying… or you snoring," he adds with a grin.

We all laugh.

Aliza just shakes her head, pretending to be annoyed. "Come on, breakfast is ready."

Chapter 20 – The Hardest Truth

Following breakfast, Elliot drives me home.

We don't talk much on the way. There's not much left to say.

I walk through the front door just before 11 a.m.

My parents are pacing in the kitchen, both looking tense. It's jarring—seeing them like this.
And for the first time in a long time, there's *actual emotion* on my dad's face.

But the second he sees me, it twists into something sharper.
Anger.

"Where have you been?" he snaps. "Do you think you can just go gallivanting off all night and not tell your mother or me where you're going?"

Before I can even respond, my mom gasps. "Oh my—what happened to your eye? Did you get into a fight?"

I exhale, trying to stay calm.

"I know I should've checked in," I say. "But… I got punched. David Bell hit me—knocked me out cold before I even had the chance to react. My friends took me to one of their houses. They watched over me. I wasn't alone."

My dad shakes his head, muttering. "Just don't let it happen again."

Then he storms out of the kitchen, drops into his recliner, and turns on the TV. Sunday football.
He'll be there for the next twelve hours, barely moving.

The Denver Broncos are already losing to the Chargers. Figures.

"You need to be more careful," my mom says flatly. "I think you're hanging around the wrong type of kids."

"You don't even know who I was with," I say, heat rising in my chest. "These 'kids'—they're the only people who've *actually* cared since Jessi died."

She opens her mouth to argue, but I keep going.

"You and Dad have changed just as much as I have. Maybe more."
My voice is shaking now. "Honestly? Getting yelled at for staying out late… it's almost *refreshing*. At least it means Dad still gives a crap."

"That's not true—" she starts.

I cut her off.

"You sit in here watching wine-soaked drama like it's therapy," I say, eyes burning. "But the truth is, we *are* one of those families. The ones people point at and whisper about. The broken ones."

I pause, chest heaving.

"I get it. I know it's my fault. I'm the reason we're this way. But I'm trying to change. I'm trying to be *better*. And I think maybe… maybe you and Dad should try too."

She doesn't say anything. Just stands there for a second.

Then she turns and leaves the kitchen—quietly crying.

Guilt tugs at me. But I don't regret saying it.
It had to be said.
All of it.

I head downstairs to my bedroom.

I strip off my hoodie, and for the first time, I catch a full look at my face in the mirror.

My right eye is a mess. Swollen. Bruised in shades of purple, blue, and black.
It'll be with me for a while.

As I get ready to shower, I empty my pockets and find something crumpled.
A folded piece of paper.

My list.

Everything is crossed off—except the last line.

Smile.

I stare at it for a long moment.
And I remember why I wrote it.

That goal. That promise.
To let myself be happy.
Even when it hurt.

I shower, clean up, and decide to stay home today. There's homework to catch up on, my room needs cleaning, and—honestly—I just need to breathe.

Saturday was magical… until it wasn't.
But Friday?

Friday was still a nightmare.

And tomorrow, I'll have to walk back into those hallways.

What will people say?

Will they pretend it didn't happen?

Will they blame me?

I just hope—for Aliza's sake—they forget. That they move on. That they don't make her relive it.

Because the truth is… it was never supposed to be about her.
She was just collateral.

And that's on me.

Chapter 21– Somewhere Between Here and Healing

6:25 a.m.

I finish getting cleaned up, grab my backpack, and head out the door just in time to catch the bus. I don't want to risk walking—I need today to start on time, on track.

I pull on the red shirt I wore Saturday night. It's the only shirt I own with any real color. It still fits, and honestly, it feels like a good choice.
I've got nicer button-downs, but I'm not sure I'm ready to revamp my whole wardrobe. This is enough for now.

New haircut. White Shirt. Red Tie. Slightly less broken attitude.
It's not perfect. But it's progress.

And for the first time in a long time… I'm actually excited for school.
I want to see Elliot. I want to see Aliza.
And—maybe selfishly—I want to see what David looks like after Saturday night.

The bus ride is quiet, but as we pull up to school, there's this strange buzz in the air. A tension. Almost like static before a storm.
I glance around. David's usual spot near the bike racks is empty.

His crew is there—but he isn't.

Aliza and Elliot are nowhere in sight either.

As the warning bell rings, I head inside, trying to focus on my goal: stay positive.
Be present. Try.

7:50 a.m.

I take a seat near the middle of my first class. Not the back row where I usually hide, but not right up front either. Just… visible.

Students start filing in, filling desks.
But something's different.

I'm not invisible anymore.

"I like your haircut, Patrick!" someone says as they sit behind me.

"How was your weekend?" another asks, genuinely.

I smile, still getting used to the idea that people are noticing me. Talking to me.
Then someone gestures to my eye.

"Sorry about your eye," they say. "Someone needs to teach David a lesson."

I laugh. "From what I hear, Aliza already did. Gave him a pretty solid shiner."

That sets off a wave of chatter.
As soon as I mention Aliza, the whole room ignites. The rumors spread like wildfire.

The rest of the morning goes about the same. Pre-class conversations. Participation. Laughter.

And me—right there in the middle of it.

Not just surviving. *Belonging.*

By lunch, I'm a little disappointed. I haven't seen Elliot. Or Aliza.
And yeah, I still haven't seen David.

Part of me wants to. Just to see the result of what happened after his cheap shot—and her right hook.

As I'm heading toward the cafeteria, I finally spot Elliot up ahead.

"Elliot! Wait up!" I jog to catch him.

He turns and grins. "Heading to lunch?"

"Yeah. Let's grab something."

We walk side by side, weaving through the crowded hall.

"Have you seen David yet?" he asks. "He's been laying low. I think he's avoiding the public eye until the black eye fades. Word is, he's telling people *you* hit him first. Says it was mutual."

I snort. "That's news to me. I may have… *accidentally* let it slip that Aliza was the one who clocked him."

Elliot bursts out laughing. "Legendary."

We reach the cafeteria doors just as I hear someone call my name.

"Patrick!"

I glance over and spot Aliza waving us over to a table full of her cheer squad friends.

I look at Elliot. "Shall we?"

He nods, and we walk over.

The conversation is light. Easy. Filled with laughter.

Her friends ask questions, trying to get to know us better. I expect it to feel awkward. It doesn't.

For the first time in what feels like forever, I feel like I *actually belong.*

Still no sign of David.

Then, over the loudspeaker:

"David Bell, please report to Principal Powell's office. David Bell."

The cafeteria buzzes instantly. Whispers fly.

"Do you think it's about the paint on Friday?" Aliza asks.

"I hope so," I say. "He deserves to be held accountable."

"I hope he gets kicked off the football team," she adds. "I don't know why I stayed with him so long. It's over. Time to move on."

The bell rings.

We clear the table and start heading our separate ways.

"Patrick—Annie's after school?" Aliza calls out.

"Absolutely."

3:00 pm

Elliot and I head straight to Annie's after school. Aliza and a few of her friends are already there, tucked into a corner booth near the window. They wave us over as we walk in.

We place our orders—shakes, fries, a couple of burgers—and join them at the table.

I sit next to Aliza. Elliot ends up across from me, right beside Brittany—a senior cheerleader who looks like she stepped out of a movie. Blonde, bright, and bold. The kind of girl who used to live in a world I didn't belong to.

But today, for some reason, I do.

We laugh, swap stories, and joke about school. I don't feel out of place. I'm part of the conversation, not just listening from the outside. The whole time, I keep wondering where David is.

"Did anyone actually see him today?" I ask. "I heard his name over the intercom at lunch, but he's been a no-show everywhere else."

Aliza thinks for a second. "Now that you mention it… no. He wasn't in chem or history either. We're in a few classes together."

"Exactly," I say. "It's weird. David's never been the hiding type. Something feels… off."

"Maybe he's finally embarrassed," Elliot offers. "Or maybe Aliza broke more than just his nose."

She grins. "I *do* hit pretty hard."

We all laugh, but I can't shake the tension building in my gut.

"Are you worried about him?" Elliot asks quietly.

"Not about *him*," I say. "Just what he might be *thinking*."

Our food comes, and the conversation shifts to lighter things. College plans. Senior skip day. Favorite Netflix shows.
It's… normal. Safe.

And for the first time in a long time, I don't feel like I'm performing.
I feel *seen*.

We hang out for a little over an hour. Around 4:15, everyone starts gathering their things.

The girls head to their cars. Elliot and I walk out together. As we reach the parking lot, I feel someone call my name.

"Patrick!"

I turn. Aliza's standing beside her car, smiling.

"Want a ride home?" she asks.

"I think Elliot was taking me," I say, glancing at him.

He elbows me hard in the side. "Are you serious?"

He leans in, lowering his voice. "Aliza Gillespie—the girl who let you sleep in her bed and basically babysat your unconscious body—is offering to drive you home, and you're going to say *no*?"

I grin.

"If you could take him," Elliot says to Aliza, "that'd be awesome. I've got errands anyway."

Liar.

I mouth *thank you* to him as I head toward her car. My nerves buzz under my skin.

Aliza is just ahead of me, unlocking the door. She's wearing skinny jeans, a fitted tee, and a leather jacket. Effortlessly gorgeous. She's the kind of girl who could roll out of bed and still make jaws drop.
She always looks put together. Polished.
Powerful.

We get in the car.

"So… where to?" she asks, flashing a playful smile.

"Home, I guess," I say, trying to keep it casual.

She raises an eyebrow. "Nah. Let's go somewhere. Just talk for a bit."

I blink. "Talk?"

"I want to know the real Patrick," she says. "Not the cafeteria version. Not the homecoming king. Just… you."

She pulls out of the lot.

My heart's in my throat.

"Okay," I say slowly. "You take me somewhere that matters to you, and I'll answer anything you want."

She grins. "Deal. It's not far, but it might take a little while. That okay?"

"More than okay."

We drive into the hills, winding through backroads I've never seen before. The town disappears in the rearview mirror. I don't ask where we're going.

She starts asking questions.

"What's your favorite thing to do? What calms you down when everything feels like too much?"

I hesitate. "I… I don't really know. I used to read a lot. I play video games sometimes. Mostly, I've been keeping to myself. Up until recently, I barely left the house. I'd go to school, go home, and that was it."

She nods, quiet but listening.

"Were you always like that?" she asks. "So closed off?"

I take a breath.

"I've always been shy," I admit. "But no, I wasn't always like this. Jessi—my sister—she brought out the lighter side of me. I was different before…"

Aliza glances over gently, finishing for me.

"Before your sister passed?"

I nod slowly, eyes fixed on the blur of trees outside the window. The air in the car shifts, heavier now—but not in a bad way. Just real.

She doesn't push.

Instead, she asks softly, "What's your favorite memory of her?"

It takes me a second to answer. My throat tightens just thinking about it. But somehow, with Aliza… it feels okay to speak.

"We used to build these crazy pillow forts," I say, smiling despite the ache. "Like, I'm talking *architectural masterpieces*. She'd use couch cushions, dining chairs, bedsheets, broomsticks—anything we could find. She'd always make me the 'engineer' and she'd be the 'creative director.' That's what she called herself."

Aliza lets out a soft laugh.

"We'd camp out in the living room for hours—flashlights, snacks, books. Sometimes she'd make me read to her, even though she was the better reader. She just liked hearing my voice, I think."

I pause. "There was this one time, we made a fort so big it wrapped around the entire couch. My mom came home and just stood there, shaking her head. She didn't even get mad. She just… smiled. Said it was the most she'd seen us get along all week."

My voice trails off. The smile fades, but not completely.

"She made everything lighter. Even the heavy stuff."

Aliza doesn't say anything right away. Just lets the silence be what it is—soft, warm, sacred.

Then she reaches over and gently places her hand on mine. No words.

Just… connection.

We talk the rest of the way. Favorite movies. Stupid fears. Comfort foods.
I forget to be nervous. I forget to be guarded.

I just… *am.*

After about twenty minutes, she slows down and turns into a narrow gravel path.

"We're here," she says, pulling into a clearing.

I look around.

There's nothing but a wide, open hill covered in tall grass, glowing green in the late afternoon sun.

No buildings. No fences. Just space. Quiet. Freedom.

It's beautiful.

Something about this place—this hill, this silence, this girl—feels new. Not loud or overwhelming. Just… safe. Like maybe what's coming next won't break me. Maybe, this time, it'll help me heal.

Chapter 22 – A Place that Heals

She hops out of the car and flashes me a grin. "We've got a bit of a hike—just over this hill. We're almost there."

Before I can respond, she's already jogging toward the giant slope. I scramble out and chase after her, my shoes crunching against gravel and grass. The hill is steeper than it looks, and pretty soon we're both slowing, breath coming harder. We pause once or twice, just long enough to catch our breath, and then keep climbing.

By the time we reach the top, I'm expecting some epic view—a sweeping valley or mountain vista. But instead, the hill levels out. It's flat up here. Quiet. A thick line of trees sits about fifty feet ahead, and a narrow path cuts between them like an invitation.

"Aliza," I say, panting. "Where are we going? Are you taking me out here to murder me?"

She laughs. "Just trust me. We're so close."

We follow the path into the woods. Branches arch above us like a tunnel, shadows stretching long with the setting sun. Up ahead, the trees begin to thin. Aliza glances back once, then bolts.

"Come on!" she yells. "Hurry!"

I sprint after her.

The trees break open—and suddenly, the earth dips again. But this time, it slopes toward a lake. Steam curls off the surface like breath in the air. The sky behind it is painted in every shade of blue, pink, and gold. The last sliver of sun rests on the horizon, seconds from vanishing.

I stop walking. I can't speak.

It's beautiful.

The wind is still. The trees are whispering. A stream trickles nearby. I close my eyes and breathe it all in—the scent of pine, earth, and something warm, almost mineral-like, carried by the steam. And beneath it all, something sweeter. Faint, familiar. Aliza's perfume—floral and soft—clings to the air like a memory I didn't know I had. It mixes with the wildness around us, grounding me in the moment.

When I open my eyes, Aliza's watching me, waiting.

"What is this place?" I finally ask. "And why does it look like the water's… smoking?"

"This," she says softly, "is Absano Reservoir. It's one of Colorado's hidden hot springs. There's a story about it—something about the Arapaho tribe believing the water had healing powers. My dad used to bring me here when I was little. And his dad brought him."

I stare out at the water, letting the silence speak for a moment.

"Thank you for sharing this with me," I say. "I wish I'd paid more attention to how we got here."

I kick off my shoes and socks and ease my feet into the water. It's warm, not scalding—like stepping into something alive. Aliza settles beside me. The last slice of sun dips below the horizon.

She leans her head gently on my shoulder, and for a moment, everything is still.

I hesitate, then slowly reach over and lace my fingers through hers. She doesn't pull away. Her hand fits into mine like it's always belonged there.

"Thank you," I say softly. "For this weekend. For being there Saturday. For… seeing me." My voice catches a little. "Elliot's always had my back, but lately, I've just felt… like I've been carrying everything alone. And then you showed up."

She lifts her head and looks at me, her eyes steady and kind.

"You're not alone anymore," she whispers.

Then, gently, her hand finds my cheek—warm, soft, grounding—and she leans in. Her lips meet mine, slow and sure, like we've both been holding our breath without realizing it.

When we finally pull apart, we don't rush to fill the silence. We just sit there, side by side, watching the stars blink to life above the water. We point out constellations, talk about nothing important, and let the quiet between us say what words can't.

Eventually, my phone buzzes.
A text from Elliot:

You alive?

We laugh under our breath, not wanting to disturb the quiet around us. The night has fully settled in, and the stars overhead feel closer than they should. It's time.

We click on our flashlights and begin the walk back through the trees, fingers still laced. The path feels shorter now. Or maybe we're just not in a rush to leave.

Back at the car, the silence between us is easy. Safe. We don't need to fill it.

When we pull up to my house, the world outside is still. The porch light glows faintly against the dark, and the street is empty. She puts the car in park but doesn't move.

I glance at her, and for a moment, I just let myself look.

"Thank you for tonight," I say, quietly but sincerely. "For all of it. I hope this is the first of… a lot more."

She smiles, soft and knowing. "I'll see you by the bike rack in the morning, Patrick Schwartz."

I smile back. "Yes, you will."

I squeeze her hand once—gentle, lingering—and then step out into the cool air. As I make my way toward the house, I pull out my phone and scroll to Elliot's name.

I step inside, heart full, ready to dial the one person who always wants to hear everything.

Chapter 23 – The Beginning of Better

I walk through the front door and glance at the clock—seven minutes past eight. My dad's already sunk into his recliner, locked in on Monday Night Football. My mom's in the kitchen, a steaming mug of tea in her hands. Her eyes are red and swollen. She's been crying—again. Probably most of the day. Ever since our talk yesterday morning. Ever since I finally said the words I've been holding in about Jessi… and the way she's been numbing the pain with wine.

I hadn't planned to say any of it, but once it started, I couldn't stop. It needed to be said. It had needed to be said for a long time.

I round the corner toward the basement stairs when her voice stops me.

"How was school?" she asks. "What did you do today?"

Her voice is soft, almost unsure. But something in it feels… different. Calmer. Steadier.

"It was good," I say, surprised that it's true. "Elliot and I went to Annie's after school. Some friends came too."

She raises an eyebrow. "You were gone for five hours?"

I hesitate. "Well… we weren't there the whole time. I went out with someone. She offered me a ride, and we ended up driving around for a while."

"She?" she asks, and there's a faint pull at the corners of her mouth—like she's trying not to smile too much.

It's only then I realize… she sounds sober. Clear. There's no slur in her voice, no fog in her words. Just curiosity. Genuine and gentle.

My face warms. "Yeah."

"Is this the same friend who helped you Saturday night?"

I nod slowly. "It is."

"What's her name?"

I try to play it cool. "Why do you assume it's a girl?"

She doesn't miss a beat. "Because of the color in your cheeks and that ridiculous grin you walked in with."

I give in. "Aliza."

"Gillespie?"

"Yeah."

Mom nods once. "Good for you, Pat. Have a good night."

"Night, Mom."

I start toward the stairs, but something makes me pause. She's still sitting there—really sitting there. Present. A little worn, but not drifting somewhere else behind her eyes. It reminds me of being fourteen, when she used to wait up just to make sure I made it home safe.

Just as I'm turning away, she takes a shaky breath.

"Pat?" she says softly. "Can I tell you something?"

I turn back. "Yeah. Of course."

She sets her mug down, both hands lingering around it like she needs its warmth to steady her.

"I made a call today," she says. "To a facility in Denver." She swallows, blinking fast but not looking away. "I'm… I'm going to go for a while. I need help. And I want to get better. I really do."

The words hang there—tentative but real. Stronger than I've heard her in months.

I don't know what to say at first. My chest tightens, not in fear this time, but something like relief—something like hope I didn't expect to feel so quickly.

"I love you," I say, quiet but steady. "Thanks for telling me."

Her eyes soften, glistening in a different way than before. "I love you too, sweetheart."

I head downstairs, holding onto that flicker of warmth a little longer than I mean to.

By the time I shut my bedroom door, the warmth from upstairs is already beginning to fade. I collapse onto my bed and grab my phone.

Elliot answers before the first ring even finishes.

"Well, well, well," he says, smirking through the phone. "Look who remembered he has a best friend."

I laugh. "Thought I'd check in. You know, see how your errands went."

He groans. "We're still calling it that?"

"Felt polite."

"Skip the formalities, Romeo. Spill it. What happened? Where'd you go? What did you and Aliza do?"

I sit up, smiling without realizing it. "We drove out somewhere. I honestly don't even know where. She took me up this hill—like, a legit hike—and then down this path to a hidden hot spring. Apparently, it's been in her family for generations. She said they used to go there when they needed to heal."

Elliot lets out a low whistle. "A secret hot spring? That's next-level. Okay, okay—never mind the scenic romance. Tell me about the talk. Like… did you open up?"

I nod, even though he can't see it. "Yeah. It was easy. Natural. She asked me real questions. Like, my favorite food, book, what calms me down when I'm overwhelmed… Stuff no one's really asked in a long time."

He's quiet for a beat. Then, "And?"

"And we talked. A lot. About everything. And then… we didn't." I pause. "After the sun went down, we just laid back and watched the stars. We didn't need to fill the silence. It was just… good."

Elliot exhales. "Dude. That's not just a date. That's, like, a soul connection."

"It felt like one," I admit softly.

There's a pause on the line. I can almost hear Elliot grinning.

"Wait… wait. Don't tell me—was there a kiss?"

I chuckle, letting my head fall back onto the pillow. "Yeah."

"No!" he practically shouts. "You're serious? Like a *real* kiss? Lips-on-lips, no-theater-makeup-involved kind of kiss?"

"Real," I say, smiling. "Soft. Simple. But… real."

"Holy crap, man," Elliot says, his voice full of disbelief and delight. "You're telling me she takes you to this secret healing lake in the middle of the mountains, you stare at the stars together in total silence, and then *kisses you*? That's—dude, that's *poetry*. That's Nicholas Sparks-level stuff."

I laugh again, a little embarrassed now. "It wasn't some dramatic, sweeping thing. It was quiet. Gentle. Like… she was saying thank you without words."

Elliot exhales, his voice softer now. "That's the part people remember the most. Not the flashy stuff. The little moments that feel big."

"Yeah," I say. "It was one of those."

"She's really into you, Pat," he says, voice softer now. "And honestly… I get it."

I pause. "You do?"

"Yeah," he says. "When you let yourself be seen—like really seen—you've got this… light. Even if it's buried deep. People notice, whether you think they do or not."

I don't say anything right away.

"It's just good to hear you like this again," he adds. "Your voice. The way you sound when you're not carrying everything on your own. It's been a long time."

"Feels like a long time since I've been this version of me," I admit.

There's a quiet moment on the line. Not awkward—just real.

"Well," Elliot says gently, "welcome back."

We say goodnight, and I hang up, the smile still lingering on my face.

I lie back on my bed, staring at the ceiling. The room is dark, quiet—except for the hum of the heater and the occasional creak of the house settling. I pull the blanket over my chest and let my thoughts drift.

I wish I could tell Jessi about tonight. About Aliza. About how—for the first time in a long time—I feel something that isn't just pain. Something light. Something real.

She'd probably tease me first. Raise an eyebrow. Call me soft.

But then she'd smile—gentle and full of fire—and she'd mean it. She always meant it.
She'd tell me I'm allowed to feel this. That it's okay to stop punishing myself for surviving.

I can almost hear her voice, soft but certain, wrapping around me like a memory I'm not ready to let go of.

"You're still my Patch," she'd say. *"Even when you forget who you are."*

That thought clings to me like warmth in winter.

I stare at the ceiling as the blue glow of my alarm clock stretches across the walls. My body sinks into the mattress. My eyes blur. My chest rises and falls.

And then… the room begins to dissolve.

The ceiling fades into clouded sky. The hum of night gives way to wind and silence. My bed slips away like a tide retreating from shore, and I fall—not in fear, but in surrender.

Into memory.

Into something waiting.

Chapter 24 – The Weight of Goodbye

I stand again at the forked path beneath the canopy of twisted trees.
The wooden sign creaks in the still air—one arrow pointing left: **Open Your Eyes**. The other pointing right: **Close Your Heart**.
The forest is hushed.
Still.
Even the wind dares not move.

Behind me, the shadow figure lingers. I can feel it. Not chasing. Not threatening. Just there—watching, waiting. For me to choose.

I think of my mom. Of her shaking hands around that tea mug. Of the quiet courage it took for her to say she was leaving—to heal. I think of how she faced her darkness instead of running from it.
I take a breath. Then another.
And I whisper, "I'm ready."

The cloaked figure lifts an arm, the sleeve falling back just enough to reveal pale, bone-thin fingers. He gestures. Not toward one path or the other—just forward. Just onward.

So I step onto the path marked **Open Your Eyes**.

The forest fades.
Rain hits my skin like cold pins. The dirt underfoot turns to soaked pavement. Sirens rise in the distance. A curve in the road. Flashing hazard lights.
And there it is.

My car. Nose-down in the ditch. Crumpled. Busted glass scattered across the asphalt like broken memories.

I'm here again.

I turn. The shadowy figure stands beside me now, silent and still.

I look around. Try to place everything.
Where were we coming from that night?
The zoo. I remember that. We were laughing. Jessi was singing with the radio. I remember the pizza place on the corner. The one we never made it to.
I glance at the direction the car is facing. It's wrong.
We were heading home. This is the opposite way.
That doesn't make sense.

I look harder. The skid marks… the ditch… the way the car is angled. It's not how I remembered.
And then it hits me.

"Wait," I say aloud, my voice barely audible over the storm. "This… this wasn't me losing control."

I step closer, heart thudding. I look at the impact point.

The passenger side.

Jessi's side.

Twisted. Caved in. The front of the car is nearly untouched.

"We were hit," I breathe. "Someone hit us…"

The figure nods. Slowly.

I whip around, eyes searching.

There.

Past the ditch. On the far embankment—another car. Or what's left of it. A pickup truck, flipped on its roof, crushed and mangled.

I stagger backward. "But no one ever said anything. They told me—I thought—I thought I was the one who—"

"You thought wrong," a voice says.

It's not the shadow. It's not in my head.

It's her.

I turn and see her.

Jessi.

Alive. Whole. Standing in the rain like a memory I wasn't ready to have back.

She's older than I remember—like the time has passed here too. But her smile? It's the same. That slightly crooked grin. That spark in her eyes. She was always the one who lit up a room just by walking in.

I can't breathe. "Jessi…"

She steps forward, slow and certain. "Hey, Patch."

I lose it. I fall to my knees in the middle of the wet road, shoulders shaking, tears indistinguishable from the rain.

"I'm so sorry," I cry. "If I hadn't been driving—if I'd just waited, if I hadn't been so careless—you'd still be here."

She kneels beside me, her hand finding mine. "Pat, listen to me. It wasn't your fault."

"I was behind the wheel."

"We had the right of way. He ran the stop sign. You were trying to protect me. You always have. Even when it wasn't your job."

I shake my head. "Dad… he said—he said he wished it was me."

Her expression softens, and she wipes a tear from my cheek. "He didn't mean it. He was broken. Still is. But he loves you, even if he forgot how to show it. And Mom… she's trying, Pat. You gave her that push."

"She's in rehab now."

"I know," Jessi whispers. "And she's going to get better. For herself. For you. For both of them."

"I don't know how to move on," I say, my voice barely more than a breath.

Jessi smiles softly. Not with pity—never with pity—but with that same fierce love that always made me feel seen.

"You already have, Patch," she says.

I blink. "What do you mean?"

"You're not the same boy who used to hide in his basement," she says gently. "You've let people in. You let Elliot pull you out of that darkness. You stood up to David. You forgave. You found joy again."

She pauses, her eyes shining.

"And then there's Aliza," she adds. "You're letting someone see you—the real you. And you're not running from it. You're showing up, even when it hurts. That's growth, Pat. That's healing."

Tears spill freely now. Not just from grief, but from something deeper. Something lighter.

"You're still here because you're supposed to be," she says, resting her forehead against mine. "You matter. And you deserve the kind of love you've been so afraid to accept."

I close my eyes and breathe her in—vanilla, spring air, and home. For the first time in a long time, I don't feel like I'm drowning.

"You're not broken," she whispers. "You're becoming."

"You have no idea how much I miss you," I whisper, my voice catching on the lump in my throat.

Jessi's eyes soften, shimmering with that same warmth I used to see every day—the kind that made the world feel safe. She lifts her hand to my face again, brushing away the tears that refuse to stop.

"I miss you too," she says, her voice barely above a breath. "But I've always been with you, Patch. Even when you couldn't see me. Even when you forgot how."

My chest tightens, a mix of grief and gratitude crashing through me.

She leans back just far enough to meet my eyes—really meet them—and the air around us stills.

"I need you to forgive yourself," she says, firm but gentle. "You didn't kill me. You loved me. With everything you had. What happened… it wasn't your fault. It was never your fault."

"But I was driving—"

"You were loving me," she interrupts, her voice trembling now. "That whole day—laughing at the zoo, singing in the car, teasing me about my terrible playlists… That was love. That's what I remember. Not fear. Not pain. Just you… being my brother."

The rain begins to slow. The sirens grow quieter, like the world is finally exhaling. Around us, the shadows soften, fading into something warm—something gold. Like sunrise breaking through the wreckage.

"I don't know how to say goodbye," I murmur, hating the finality in the word.

"You don't have to," she says, smiling through her tears. "I'm not leaving. Not really."

She rests her forehead against mine for one final breath.

"When you need me," she whispers, "you'll know where to find me. I'll always be at the fork. Just listen for the quiet. Just look for the light."

And then… she's gone.

Not ripped away. Not vanished in pain. Just… gone. Like a song ending gently. Like peace.

Chapter 25 – A Different Version of Us

I wake up and a sense of calmness washes over me. A sense of relief knowing the truth behind the accident. Having a calmness of feeling that Jessi doesn't blame me. These dreams, were they just that, a dream? Was the interaction real between Jessi and I? It felt real? It felt as though we had a conversation, and I remember it all. Was it something more?

As I roll out of bed, after sleeping in, with it being a weekend, and I follow my same routine of showering, getting dressed and heading up stairs for breakfast. As I reach the doorway from the basement, I see my dad sitting at the kitchen table, as if waiting for someone or something. I haven't even seen him in almost a week and a half.

"Morning." He says. I am shocked, this is the most he has spoken to me in almost a year.

"Good morning." I reply. As I think, I prepare my cereal, I am lost in thought to the last time my father spoke to me willingly. The first morning, which I was home from the hospital following the incident.

I was woken up from loud sounds of crashing in the room next to me. Sore and stiff, I stretch my limbs. I get out of bed and for the last time, I walk into Jessi's room right beside mine. I see my dad, red faced, full of anger, chucking meaningless trinkets against the wall. They immediately shatter on impact spraying glass shards across the room. The room was in shambles, broken glass and objects covered the carpet. The memory of Jessi evaporating from the room like a wisp of steam. The anger and rage uncontrolled seeping out through my father. If this were a cartoon there would've been a train whistle and smoke coming from his ears.

"Dad, what are you doing." I begin. "Are you okay?"

He simply glares at me. The hatred I feel from his eyes is overpowering. His silence is deafening. The deep inhales and sharp exhales nearly swallow me up.

"What's wrong with you?" I ask.

"What's wrong? What's wrong? You killed your sister." He yells. "Let's be honest, you were driving the car. You killed Jessi. That's what's wrong. This is all your fault. She's not here because of you."

Tears well up in my eyes. A knife stabbing into my heart. I know I will never see her again. God, please take me instead. Bring back my sister and take me in her place. The world was a better place with her in it and it needs her back. Take me. I remain silent and like a lost puppy look longingly at my father unsure of what to do or say. I'm too stunned to speak. To broken to move.

"It's not fair." He says angrily. "I wish it would've been you."

And like dish of fine china dropping to the floor, I shatter to a million pieces at those words. Irreparable damage has been done. My relationship with my father will never be the same. My father wishes I were dead. My father, if Jessi were still here and I were in her place, wouldn't even miss me. Those were the last words my father spoke to me until just now. "I wish it would've been you."

I'm sucked out of my own head, when for a second or a 3rd time I finally register my name is being called.

"Pat….Pat." My dad calls.

"Yeah." It's all I can summon, after remembering the last conversation we had.

"With your mom being gone and you making the changes you have, I just wanted to say," he pauses, "I'm sorry. You don't deserve to be treated like you have been. I should've been here to support you more."

Shocked, unsure of how to respond, I ask, "Do you remember the last thing you said to me? The reason I moved to the basement and away from Jessi's room? Do you remember the last words you spoke to me in 9 months? Do you!"

"I was angry." He starts.

I cut him off and don't let him finish. "We all were. I was one day out of the hospital." I say starting to cry. "One day out of the hospital and you told me you wished it were me. You know what? I did too. I pleaded with God that I wouldn't wake up. I pleaded that this this would be a bad dream and it would go back to normal. I begged and bargained that he would swap us places. He didn't grant me that mercy. I'm sorry it wasn't me. I am sorry you lost Jessi and all you have is me. A disappointment. I'm sorry that because of me, mom became an alcoholic and is now in rehab for it. I am sorry I ruined our perfect family. You can blame me all you want, but I know the truth you and mom both failed me. When I needed you most."

"Pat." He starts.

I cut him off, "No, its my turn to talk. It wasn't my fault, we were hit. We had the right of way and we were hit." The tears are flowing and I finally feel a sense of relief wash over me. The weight of my father's anger washed away. My guilt of the accident gone.

"You're right." He admits. "What I said wasn't right and no boy should ever hear those words from his father. I miss Jessi, but it wasn't right for me to wish you in her place." He has a single tear streaming down his cheek. " The last several months, I haven't talked to you, not because I was angry with you, but because I was so disappointed in myself. I had said, unspeakable words. I had done irreparable damage to my relationship with you. I didn't speak to you, because of what I had said. Because of the damage that I had done." He wipes his cheek and pauses. "These last few months and the changes I have seen you make….I have been so proud of you. I am sorry son. I hope one day you can forgive me." He stands, pushes in his chair and heads to the living room. The conversation is over.

Can the damage ever be repaired? I wasn't sure. I headed back downstairs, to watch shows or play games until I heard from Elliot. I decide to clean my room and I turn on my favorite show that I have seen over and over just to fill the void. In the episode of Ted Lasso I am watching, a psychic teaches Richmond owner, Rebecca, the art of Kintsugi. The art of fixing broken things with gold. The psychic says, "The idea is that we embrace the flaws and imperfections and create something much stronger and more beautiful."

I look at the discussion that I just had with my father, his apology. My regrets and longings finally boiling over. My father bearing his emotions. Me telling him how he made me feel. Our relationship has been broken. My accident…Jessi's death has shattered a lot of relationships and memories. None of us will ever be as we once were. We will never be whole again, but, maybe, we could repair our lives in a Kintsugi way. I realize what needs to be done. I need to be the bigger person and take the next steps.

I run up stairs as fast as I can skipping steps on the way and my dad is sitting in his recliner reading the newspaper. "Dad, I'm sorry for what I said. I shouldn't have yelled at you. I was angry and hurt by what you said."

"I get it Pat. I was also angry and hurt when I said what I did." He pauses. " I know you probably can't forgive me, but I am sorry for saying I wish it was you. It wasn't fair and I know, the accident, wasn't your fault. I'm sorry Pat. From now on, I will be around as much as I can. Especially now that your mom will be gone the next few weeks."

"Dad."

"Yeah, bud."

"How about some milkshakes after school?" I ask. "Just us."

He looks up from the paper, a flicker of something warm returning to his face. "You're buying?"

I grin. "Don't push it."

He chuckles—a real, quiet laugh. "Alright. After school, then."

I nod and turn toward the stairs. It's not a full repair, not yet. But maybe, just maybe, it's the first crack filled with gold.

School moves in a blur. Not because it's particularly exciting—just... different. I feel lighter. Not fixed, not healed, but like something cracked open and let a little light in.

At lunch, Elliot's already at the table when I sit down. Aliza slides in beside me, nudging me with her shoulder.

"You good?" she asks.

I nod. "Yeah. I actually... talked to my dad this morning."

Elliot raises an eyebrow. "Like, real conversation talk? Or the usual ghostly grunt from across the house?"

"Real talk," I say. "He apologized."

They both pause. It's the kind of pause that holds weight.

"That's huge," Aliza says.

"It felt... like something I've been waiting months to hear," I admit. "We're going to Annie's tonight. Just the two of us."

Elliot grins. "Look at you, making moves. Emotional growth and burgers? That's next-level."

We laugh.

The rest of the school day passes quietly. Every now and then, I catch myself thinking about the morning—my dad's voice, his words. The look in his eyes when he said he was proud of me. I can't remember the last time I heard that.

After the final bell rings, I ride the bus home. Aliza has cheer, Elliot has to work, and honestly… I'm okay being alone for a bit. The house is still when I walk in. The usual sounds—TV in the background, Mom's wine glass clinking against the table—aren't there. Just the hum of the fridge and the creak of the floor beneath my feet.

I head down to my room, drop my bag, and change out of my school clothes. The dream from last night still lingers. Jessi's voice. Her forgiveness. The feeling of her arms around me. I close my eyes for just a second and hear her again.

"You have to love yourself enough to live."

I don't know if I believe it yet. But I want to.

When I come back upstairs, Dad's already by the front door, keys in hand.

"You ready?" he asks.

"Yeah," I say, grabbing my coat.

We don't talk much in the car, but it's not awkward. It's quiet, like we're both still adjusting to this new version of us.

When we pull up to Annie's, it looks the same as always—neon sign flickering, the smell of fries and grilled onions wafting out the door. But somehow, it feels different tonight.

We grab a booth near the back, the one Jessi used to claim as "hers." I glance at it and then back at my dad. He notices too, but doesn't say anything.

We order our usual. I get a bacon cheeseburger and a strawberry milkshake. He gets a double cheeseburger with grilled mushrooms and a chocolate malt.

Halfway through the meal, he finally speaks.

We sit across from each other in the warm glow of the diner, the smell of burgers and vanilla ice cream swirling around us like something familiar—something safe. The clink of silverware and quiet hum of conversation fill the background, but here, in this little booth, it feels like the world has paused just long enough to breathe.

My dad sets his cup down gently, both hands wrapped around it like he's not sure what to do with them.

"I'm really glad you came," he says softly, eyes not quite meeting mine. "I've wanted to do this for a long time… just sit with you. Be your dad again."

I nod slowly, my throat tightening. "Me too."

We don't say much for a while. We just sip our milkshakes and pick at our fries, letting the quiet speak for us. And for the first time in a long time, the silence between us doesn't feel heavy.

I glance over at him, at the lines on his face, the tiredness behind his eyes. But also the softness that's starting to return—the father I used to know, flickering back to life.

"Do you think we'll ever get back to the way things were?" I ask, my voice barely above a whisper.

He pauses, thoughtful. Then, gently, "No. I don't think we're supposed to."

I look down, unsure how to take that.

"But," he continues, "that doesn't mean we can't build something new. Something better. Maybe it won't ever be like before, but… we can still be us again. Just… a different version."

I swallow hard. "I'd like that."

"So would I," he says. "More than you know."

He leans back, clears his throat like he's trying to swallow everything he didn't say for the last nine months. Then, quietly, he says,
"I meant what I said, Pat. I'm proud of you."
It's not a hug. It's not a hand squeeze. But coming from my dad?
It's a crack of sunlight.

Chapter 26 – "Deadlines and Dreams"

December settled in without asking permission. One day we were walking home under crisp golden leaves, the next we were waking up to frost-lined windows and college application reminders on every hallway bulletin board.

It felt like the whole school was suddenly sprinting toward something—deadlines, dreams, dorm life—while I was just trying to keep up.

Aliza texted me after school.
Meet me at Annie's? I need chili fries and life advice.

I got there first, our usual booth by the window already warmed by the afternoon sun. A minute later, she slid into the seat across from me, cheeks flushed pink from the cold, her laptop hugged to her chest.

She set it down with a small sigh, flipping it open. "So… I kind of heard from a few more schools."

I raised an eyebrow. "Yeah?"

She nodded, tucking a strand of hair behind her ear. "It's weird. I should be excited—USC, ASU, Boulder… even Denver offered something. I should be thrilled, right?"

"That's amazing, Aliza," I said. And I meant it. "Seriously. You worked hard for that."

"I know," she said quietly. "It just… makes everything feel more real. Like everything's speeding up and I'm trying to be excited, but I'm also kind of terrified."

"That makes two of us."

She smiled, grateful—not just for the validation, but maybe for not having to pretend everything was perfect.

"What about you?" she asked, reaching for a fry. "Any schools on your radar?"

I shrugged. "A couple. Smaller ones. I've thought about education… or psychology. Just something where I can help people. I don't know if that makes sense."

"It does," she said, without hesitation. "It makes all the sense in the world."

She smiled, then looked down at her drink. "Yeah, I've thought about nursing. Pediatric care, maybe. I've always liked the idea of helping kids, especially the ones who don't get a fair shot."

I nodded. "That sounds like you."

She stirred her straw around in her drink for a second, thinking. "You know what you'd be amazing at?" she said, setting her drink down. "Patrick Schwartz, Child Life Specialist."

I blinked. "That's… a thing?"

She nodded. "It is. They work in hospitals, mostly with kids—helping them process trauma, grief, medical stuff, all of it. They use play therapy, art, even just being there to explain what's happening in a way that makes sense. They support families too. Emotionally. Mentally. It's not just a job, it's... heart work. And it's exactly the kind of thing you'd be incredible at."

"Me?"

"Yeah. I mean, you've been through more than most people our age can even imagine, and somehow, you're still here—still showing up, still trying. And when you talk to people, Pat… you really talk to them. You listen. I think you'd be good at something like that."

I sat back for a moment, letting it sink in.
No one had ever said something like that to me before.

"I don't know," I said, my voice quieter now. "I guess I've always wanted to help people, I just… never thought I could turn everything I've been through into something *useful*. Something good."

"Well," she said, nudging her foot against mine beneath the table, "maybe it's time you did."

Patrick sat back and stared out the diner window. Snow had started to fall—soft, silent flakes catching the glow of the neon "OPEN" sign in the glass.

He didn't speak right away.

"I don't know," he said finally, his voice lower. "Maybe it sounds dumb, but… the idea of helping kids like that—kids going through loss, or trauma—there's something about it that feels… right. Like maybe everything I've been through could actually mean something. Could actually help someone else."

He paused, swallowing down a lump in his throat. His fingers tapped lightly against the side of his milkshake glass.

"But at the same time…" His eyes stayed fixed on the snowfall. "I'm scared. Not just about college, or picking a path. I'm scared of losing you. And Elliot. Of everything changing."

Aliza didn't say anything right away. She let the silence breathe.

"I mean, in just a few months, we'll all be going our separate ways. New schools, new cities, new lives. And I don't know if I'm ready for that. I'm just starting to feel… okay again. And now it's all about to change."

I turned toward her. "What if I lose both of you? What if this—" I motioned between, to the table, the diner, the familiar comfort of it all—"what if this doesn't survive whatever comes next?"

Aliza reached across the table, her hand finding mine.

"We might end up in different places, Pat," she said softly. "I'm not gonna lie to you and say everything will stay exactly the same—because it won't. And yeah, that's scary. Terrifying, even."

She squeezed my hand, just enough to let it land.

"But here's what I know: You'll always have me. And Elliot. No matter where we end up, that doesn't go away. The memories, the late-night talks, the bike rack mornings… they don't just vanish because we graduate."

She smiled, a little wistfully. "We still have now. And right now, I'm here. Elliot's here. We're in your corner, for as long as you'll have us."

I looked at her, eyes glassy.

"I'm not ready to let go," he said.

"You don't have to," she whispered. "Not yet. We've still got time."

We finished our fries and talked about everything else—Elliot's plans, the last football game, the fact that school felt like it was speeding up and slowing down all at once.

And before I knew it… December was almost gone. The holidays crept in with soft snow and a quiet kind of warmth I hadn't felt in a long time.

I sat at my desk and pulled out the crumpled assignment sheet Mrs. Carson gave us back in the fall. The one I couldn't touch when she first handed it out. The one that asked us to write about a memory—something real, something personal.

Back then, I thought: *There's nothing I want to remember.* But now… it's different.

I wrote about Jessi. About the day at the zoo. About her flip-flop kicked up on the dash and the way she sang the wrong lyrics like she owned them. About how her hair danced in the wind. About the moment before the light turned red.

I wrote about how alive she was.
And how fast that life disappeared.

This time, I didn't hold back. I didn't try to make it sound poetic. I just told the truth.

Not just the parts that hurt—but the ones that glowed, too.
The ones I'd buried because remembering used to feel like punishment.

But maybe… remembering her isn't the nightmare. Maybe the nightmare was pretending I didn't still carry her with me.

The house was quiet—just the scratch of my pencil and the low tick of the kitchen clock.

I slipped the paper into my backpack, stood up, and wandered upstairs and into the kitchen.

Dad was there, fiddling with the coffee maker even though it was well past dinner. He looked up, surprised.

"Hey, bud. Couldn't sleep?"

I shrugged. "Just… thinking."

He poured himself a mug and nodded toward the seat across from him. "Sit with me a minute?"

I did.

The silence between us wasn't heavy like it used to be. It felt... open. Like something waiting to be said.

"You've changed a lot this year, Pat," he said quietly. "I can see it. And I'm proud of you."

I looked down at my hands, my throat tightening.

He cleared his throat. "So, uh… what are you thinking for next year? College, career… that stuff."

I hesitated. "Actually… I was discussing this today with Aliza."

He waited, patient.

"I want to help people," I said. "She told me about something called a Child Life Specialist. It's someone who helps kids in hospitals—kids going through really hard stuff. They help the families too. Just… make sure no one feels alone."

Dad's expression softened. "You'd be good at that."

I let out a shaky breath. "I hope so. I think I just want to be the person I could have needed."

He reached across the table and placed his hand over mine. His skin was rough, calloused from years of work—but the gesture was gentle.

"You already are," he said. "But if that's what you want… I'm behind you all the way."

I looked up. And for the first time in a long time, there wasn't distance between us. Just understanding.

"Thanks, Dad," I said softly.

He gave my hand a squeeze, then let go. "Get some sleep," he said. "Tomorrow's a new day."

And for once, that didn't sound like a threat.

It sounded like hope.

Chapter 27 – Moments We Don't Get Back

Christmas break had a way of slowing everything down. No alarms. No deadlines. Just frost on the windows and that peaceful kind of quiet only winter seems to know how to hold.

Elliot texted the group chat that morning:
Bundle up. We're going sledding. 1:00. The Big Hill. No excuses.

By 1:15, we were all standing at the top of Crestview Hill, a weathered plastic sled under each arm and not a single adult in sight. Aliza was wearing three layers and still shivering. Erica was trying to convince Elliot to use the tandem sled with her, which was really just a ploy to make him fall on his face—and it worked.

I hadn't laughed that hard in months.

The four of us spent the next two hours chasing childhood. We launched ourselves down the hillside like we didn't have a care in the world—because for once, maybe we didn't. There were no bullies here, no report cards, no grief trailing behind us like a shadow. Just fresh snow, raw laughter, and gravity doing its thing.

No one talked about college applications. No one mentioned deadlines or acceptance letters or where we might end up next fall. It all felt distant—something waiting quietly beyond the hill, polite enough to let us have this moment.

And so, we kept racing the cold, flinging snowballs at each other with frozen fingers, collapsing into snowdrifts like the world hadn't asked us to grow up yet. Erica caught Elliot mid-wipeout and laughed so hard she fell, too. Aliza tried to build a snow ramp, and I volunteered to be the test subject—which, in hindsight, was a poor decision but great for comedy.

I don't know if it was the cold or the company or the simple fact that no one had a reason to check their phones, but the afternoon felt untouched. Like we'd carved out this little corner of time just for ourselves.

For once, the world didn't feel like it was moving too fast.

Just this hill. Just us. Just now.

By the time we were frozen to our bones and laughing through red cheeks, Elliot suggested Annie's for hot chocolate. No one argued.

We crammed into our booth, boots dripping, noses pink. Aliza tucked her legs under herself, stealing sips of my cocoa while pretending hers was too cold to drink.

Somewhere between talking about ridiculous family holiday traditions and arguing over whether *Die Hard* was a Christmas movie (it is), the topic of gifts came up.

"You guys already get stuff for each other?" Elliot asked, casually. "Because I'm panicking a little."

Erica grinned. "I've had yours since Thanksgiving. But no pressure."

Aliza smirked at me. "You better be taking notes."

I laughed nervously. "I was, uh, just about to start thinking about that."

After we dropped the girls off, Elliot and I ended up circling back to his house, both of us stalling in the car a little longer than we needed to.

"We're kind of pathetic," he said. "Last-minute shopping for the girls we talk to every day."

"Very pathetic," I agreed. "But also... kind of perfect?"

He nodded. "Let's make it count."

We drove through town, chasing open stores and sparks of inspiration, not really knowing what we were looking for—just that we wanted whatever we picked to mean something.

Something real.

We were sitting on a bench outside a bookstore that smelled like cinnamon and indecision.

Elliot was flipping through a comic he definitely wasn't going to buy. I was scrolling through my phone, aimlessly at first, until something stopped me. A photo.

It was from that night.

The hot spring.

The one Aliza took me to, when everything in my life felt heavy—when just being near her made things feel a little less broken. I must have taken it just before we left, almost forgetting I had.

The steam curling up into the star-splashed sky. The reflection of pine trees rippling in the water. The soft pink of twilight still holding onto the edges of the lake.

My chest tightened.

I stared at the screen for a long time, and then turned it toward Elliot.

"What if… this is the gift?" I asked quietly. "I print it. Frame it. Write something under the photo. Something real."

He nodded, serious for once. "That's it, man. That's the one."

We swung by the print shop next, and while the photo processed, I found a simple white frame and a soft gray marker. On the bottom border, I wrote:

"Here, you healed me. Here, I found peace. —Patrick"

I stared at the words for a moment before capping the pen. It wasn't just a caption.

It was the truth.

Elliot read it and let out a low whistle. "Dang, man. You're gonna make the rest of us look bad."

I shrugged, smiling. "Just trying to keep up."

"Alright," he said, clapping his hands. "Your turn's done. My turn to shine."

We ended up at the craft store, where Elliot bought a blank wall calendar and a pack of colored pencils. "Twelve months," he said proudly. "Each page gets one custom drawing, one ridiculous quote, and one memory. The ultimate Erica and Elliot scrapbook-slash-calendar-slash-masterpiece."

I shook my head. "She's either gonna love that… or frame it as psychological evidence."

"She'll laugh," he said, grinning. "And that's the goal."

By the time we got back in the car, snow was starting to fall. Not heavy—just enough to coat the windshield in a soft blur.

"You think they'll like them?" I asked.

"I think," Elliot said, buckling his seatbelt, "they'll know we care. And that's the point, right?"

I nodded. "That's the point."

We pulled out onto the road, headlights cutting through the snow. Christmas was only a few days away.

And for once, it felt like something to look forward to.

Elliot dropped me off just after dusk, the car still dusted in snow, the laughter from the hill echoing faintly in my ears. The porch light flickered as I stepped onto the front walk, kicking off some of the slush from my boots.

That's when I noticed it—one envelope sitting alone in the mailbox, no return address. Just my name written in neat, familiar handwriting.

Inside the house, I headed straight to my room, fingers numb as I tore the seal.

I sat on the edge of my bed and unfolded the letter.

Patrick,

I don't know where to begin. I don't know how to say I'm sorry in a way that feels big enough for what I've done—or not done.

These past seven months… I've been lost. I let my grief become a storm, and I let it carry me so far away from everything that mattered. From you. I shut down, disappeared, poured my pain into a bottle and tried to convince myself I was coping. But I wasn't. I was drowning. And the worst part is… I didn't see that I was pulling you down with me.

I drank because I didn't want to feel. I numbed myself because the pain of losing Jessi was too sharp, too constant, too unbearable. But in trying to escape that pain, I forgot the most important truth—I still had a son who was hurting too. A son who needed me. A son I abandoned in the name of survival.

Patrick, I've missed so much. Not just school pictures and open houses. I've missed your laughter. Your heartbreak. Your healing. I've missed who you're becoming. And I hate that I wasn't there to witness it.

I'm writing this from a place that's teaching me how to heal. Not just how to stop drinking, but how to live again. How to feel. How to be present. It's not easy. There are days I want to quit, days I still feel like I've ruined everything beyond repair. But then I think of you.

I think of the boy who used to leave me sticky notes on the fridge telling me to have a good day. The boy who stayed strong when the rest of us fell apart. The boy who didn't deserve to carry the weight of our brokenness on his back.

You've always been stronger than you know. And I hope, more than anything, that you can find a way to let go of the guilt that was never yours to begin with. What happened that night… it wasn't your fault. It was a tragedy. A heartbreaking, unfair tragedy. But it wasn't yours to bear alone.

I won't be home for Christmas this year, and that breaks my heart. But I'll be thinking of you every second. And when I do come home, I want to do it right. I want to be a mom again—your mom. The one you've always needed. The one you deserve.

Please don't give up on me. I'm trying, Patrick. Really trying.

I love you more than you'll ever know.

Always,
Mom

Chapter 28 – Forever Fifteen

It's Christmas day. The morning is quiet. Not silent—but a kind of peaceful quiet that asks for reverence. Snow coats everything in soft white. The cemetery looks untouched, like the world pressed pause just long enough for me to catch my breath.

I walk the path I've taken only once before. It feels different now. Not heavier, not lighter—just real. My boots crunch softly as I stop in front of the grave marker.

Jessi Anne Schwartz
Forever Fifteen. Forever loved.

I kneel, brushing away the snow covering her name, and pull the folded paper from my coat pocket—the one I wrote a few nights ago but couldn't bring myself to read aloud until now.

Dear Jessi,

I don't know where to begin.

This is my first Christmas without you, and it feels... quieter. Not just in the house, but inside me too. Like there's a song missing its melody. A chair that no one dares to sit in. A laugh that used to echo in the walls but doesn't anymore.

I came here today because I needed you to know—I haven't stopped thinking about you. Not for one second.

There were days I hated myself for living when you didn't. I'd wake up and wish I hadn't. I'd look in the mirror and see the boy who failed you. And for a while… I believed I did.

But something's changed. Maybe it was the dreams. Maybe it was Aliza. Maybe it was you. But somewhere in the middle of the pain, I started to remember you not just as the girl I lost, but as the sister who loved me fiercely. The one who always called me Patch when no one else could get away with it.

You showed me how to laugh. You gave me permission to cry. And when I forgot who I was… you never did.

I'm still figuring it all out, but I'm trying, Jess. I'm really trying. I've started to see pieces of myself again—pieces that don't feel broken anymore. Not perfect. But maybe, just maybe, something worth rebuilding.

I met someone. Her name's Aliza. She's brave and stubborn and kind. She makes me feel like I'm allowed to hope again. Like maybe I deserve good things, even if I still don't always believe it.

And Mom? She's in rehab. She's getting better. Slowly, but it's real this time. And Dad… we talked. Really talked. We're not there yet, but we're not nothing either. I think you'd be proud of that.

I guess what I really want to say is... thank you.

For being my best friend. For being my sister. For loving me when I couldn't even look at myself.

I still miss you. Every hour. Every heartbeat. But it's not all sharp edges anymore. Sometimes, it's soft. Sometimes, it's even sweet.

I carry you with me, Jessi Anne. In the snow. In the silence. In every step forward.

And I hope—wherever you are—you can feel how much I love you.

Always,

Patch

I fold the letter carefully, smoothing the creases with my fingers, then set it beside the headstone—tucked just beneath the small bouquet of white pine and winterberries I brought from home. The wind brushes past my coat, gentle and cold, like a breath from someplace far away.

I kneel for a moment longer, resting my hand against the edge of the stone. The name etched into the granite doesn't feel so final anymore. It feels like a doorway. Like she's not gone, not really—just waiting somewhere I can't reach yet.

"Merry Christmas, Jess," I whisper, my voice catching on the words.

A single snowflake lands on the stone and melts almost instantly.

I stay there for a few more seconds, breathing in the quiet, trying to memorize the peace of this moment—the kind that doesn't erase the pain, but holds it gently. The kind Jess would have wrapped me in if she could.

Then I rise slowly, brushing the snow from my knees. I take one last look, not to say goodbye, but to say *I'll carry you with me.*

And I do.

I walk back toward the car with the ache still in my chest… but also something else. Something softer. Something that feels a little like healing.

Blake Collins

Chapter 29 – A Season for Remembering

Christmas morning was quieter than usual.

No Jessi sneaking into my room at 5 a.m. to beg me to open presents. No cinnamon rolls in the oven. No holiday playlist echoing off the walls. Just me and Dad, each nursing a cup of cocoa and avoiding eye contact across the living room.

The silence stretched until I finally cleared my throat.

"So... Aliza's family invited us to dinner tonight."

Dad looked up from his mug, brow raised. "Us?"

"Yeah. Her parents asked if we'd join them. Said it would mean a lot to her." I paused. "And to me."

He shifted in his chair, running a hand across the back of his neck. "I don't know, Pat. I don't want to impose. And... I've never even met them."

"You don't need to know them," I said gently. "You just need to show up—for me."

He looked at me then, really looked. And for a second, I saw something flicker in his eyes—uncertainty, maybe, or fear. But underneath it, something softer.

"I've missed a lot," he said, voice low. "If this helps make up for even a little of that... then yeah. Let's go."

By six o'clock, we were standing on the Gillespies' porch, Dad nervously adjusting the sleeves of his nicest button-up—the one I made him wear.

The door swung open before we could knock. Aliza's mom greeted us with a warm smile and a tray of peppermint bark.

"You must be Brent," she said, already ushering us inside. "Patrick talks about you all the time."

He blinked. "Hopefully not *all* the time."

Laughter broke the tension.

The Gillespie house smelled like baked ham and rosemary and fresh rolls. The tree sparkled in the corner of the living room, and Aliza waved from the couch, cheeks flushed from the warmth of the fire—or maybe from seeing me.

Dinner was loud and full of overlapping stories. I kept sneaking glances at Dad, half-waiting for him to retreat into himself. But something unexpected happened. He started talking. Then laughing. Then telling a story about how Jessi used to cover the living room in tinsel and drive him crazy.

Aliza's dad leaned in, genuinely invested. Her mom wiped away a tear, nodding with the kind of understanding only a mother could give.

I'd never seen my dad like that before—open, real, present.

And for the first time in a long time, it didn't feel like we were guests in someone else's joy. It felt like we belonged in it too.

After dinner, Aliza tugged my sleeve and pulled me toward the den. The lights were dim, and the tree cast a soft golden glow over the room. A few unopened presents remained under the tree, tucked between ribbons and sprigs of pine.

She reached under the lowest branch and pulled out a neatly wrapped box, tied with simple twine.

"Okay," she said, smiling. "Your turn first."

I sat down on the edge of the couch and peeled back the paper. Beneath it was a leather-bound journal—dark brown, soft, worn-looking in the best kind of way. On the cover, pressed into the leather in quiet, gold lettering, were the words:

For the thoughts you can't say out loud,
the memories you want to keep,
and the moments that still hurt but matter.

Inside was a pen, secured with a small ribbon. Tucked into the first page, on a small card, she had written:

"Write it all down, Pat.
The pain, the joy, the in-between.
Your story matters.
– A."

I ran my fingers over the engraving, my throat tightening.

"I didn't want to assume you'd even use it," she said softly. "But I thought… maybe you'd want a place to put everything. When it gets too heavy to carry alone."

I swallowed hard. "It's perfect."

She smiled and leaned into me, forehead against my shoulder.

I bent down and picked up the small, unevenly wrapped present I'd brought in earlier that evening. "Okay," I said, holding it out.

"It's your turn, hopefully you like it."

She took it gently, her fingers brushing mine, then sat cross-legged on the carpet. I sat beside her as she unwrapped it, slow and careful, like she already knew it was something that mattered.

Her breath caught the second the paper fell away.

It was the photo. The one I'd taken that night at the hot spring—our hidden place. The night that cracked something open in me. Framed in simple wood, and beneath it, in my handwriting:

"Here, I started to heal.
Here, you helped me find my way back."
– Patrick

She stared at it for a long moment, just running her thumb along the frame like it might disappear if she blinked.

Then she looked up at me, eyes glistening. "You remembered."

I swallowed, suddenly unsure of everything except this. "I never forgot."

She frame the frame against the wall carefully, then leaned forward and wrapped her arms around me—tight and unshaken.

Just when I thought we were finished, she reached behind the tree one more time and pulled out a slim rectangular box wrapped in pale gold paper.

"Okay," she said with a little grin. "One last one."

I raised an eyebrow as she handed it to me. "You really didn't have to—"

"I know," she interrupted, eyes gleaming. "Just open it."

I peeled back the paper and lifted the lid. Inside was a button-down shirt—canary yellow, soft cotton, crisp collar.

"Yellow?" I asked, holding it up, my face somewhere between confusion and curiosity.

She laughed. "For when you're ready to broaden your wardrobe of colors. I figured you've worn that red shirt enough times for Jessi's stamp of approval."

I glanced at the shirt again, the vibrant color nearly glowing in the soft light. "I'm not sure if yellow is me."

"It can be," she said, her voice warm. "Maybe it already is. Maybe one day, you'll feel ready to give yellow a shot."

I looked at her—really looked. Then smiled. "Thank you. For everything."

We settled onto the couch, the soft amber glow of the Christmas tree casting patterns across her cheeks. The room was quiet—just the faint hum of distant carols and the crackle of a candle flickering near the window.

Aliza looked at me again, this time more gently. "Did you get to see her today?" she asked. "Jessi?"

I nodded, my eyes falling to my hands. "Yeah… I went to the cemetery this morning."

Aliza didn't say anything. She just waited.

"It was the first time since the funeral," I admitted. "I brought her a letter. Told her about you. About Mom. About everything I've been trying to change."

Her hand slid into mine, soft and steady.

"I told her I miss her," I added. "But I think… for the first time, it didn't feel like drowning. It felt like remembering."

Aliza tilted her head, her voice almost a whisper. "Remembering?"

I swallowed, my throat tight. "For a long time after the accident, I begged God to take me instead. Every night, I pleaded with Him to undo it. I would've traded anything—my life for hers, a thousand times over. And every morning, I woke up angry that He hadn't listened."

I paused, the words heavier than I expected. "But today… standing at her grave, I realized I was glad He didn't. Because of you."

Aliza's eyes shimmered, but she didn't look away. She just squeezed my hand, like she understood without needing to speak.

She leaned closer. "Okay then… tell me. What do you remember about Jessi? About Christmas?"

I let out a slow breath, the kind that shakes a little on the way out.
"There was this one year," I began, smiling despite the ache. "We were probably seven and nine. Jessi got a

karaoke machine for Christmas—pink, glittery, the whole works. She forced me into singing duets with her all morning. I was mortified. My mom has a picture of me mid-verse, in Batman pajamas, holding the mic like it was radioactive."

Aliza chuckled softly. "I would pay money to see that photo."

"She wouldn't let me stop until we nailed *Winter Wonderland* in perfect harmony," I said. "And the thing is… we didn't. Not even close. We were off-key, loud, ridiculous. But she loved it. She danced around the living room like we were on stage at Radio City."

I paused, the memory wrapping itself around me like a blanket—equal parts warmth and ache.
"I remember her laugh that morning," I said, more quietly now. "I remember how she looked at me like we were the whole world."

Aliza leaned her head against mine.
"She still would," she whispered. "If she could."

We didn't say anything for a while after that.
Just sat there, side by side, while the tree lights blinked slowly around us and the echoes of old songs—ones only we remembered—played somewhere far off in the corners of our hearts.

Chapter 30 – Bridges and Blueprints

The house had never felt quieter—or cleaner. Dad paced the living room for the third time, adjusting cushions that were already straight. I stood near the front door, staring at my phone, counting down minutes that felt longer than hours.

"You think she's nervous?" Dad asked, finally breaking the silence.

I looked up, sliding my phone into my pocket. "Probably as nervous as we are."

He nodded, sighing deeply. "Right."

Headlights washed across the front window, and my pulse quickened. A moment later, the door opened, and Mom stepped inside.

She paused in the entryway, eyes carefully moving around the room as if trying to recognize a place she'd dreamed of returning to but found slightly altered.

"Hey," she said softly, smiling hesitantly.

"Hi, Mom," I replied, stepping forward to hug her. She hugged me tightly, holding on a beat longer than usual. When we pulled apart, her eyes shone brighter than I remembered.

"Welcome home," Dad said quietly, stepping forward. They embraced cautiously, both unsure and hopeful. "We've missed you."

We tried to make dinner feel normal.

It wasn't.

Conversation came in slow bursts—safe topics like the weather, school, and what TV shows we'd missed. Dad asked about her time in Denver, and she answered in vague, careful terms. No specifics. No pain. Just enough to say, *I'm trying.*

And maybe that was enough for tonight.

At one point, Mom laughed at something Dad said, and the sound made me freeze. I hadn't heard it in so long, it startled me. But it was real. Not the tired, hollow kind of laugh she used to fake. This one had life in it.

After dinner, I helped clear the plates while Dad and Mom lingered at the table. I caught them talking quietly, heads tilted toward one another like they used to when they thought Jessi and I weren't paying attention. Something about it made my chest ache—in a good way.

Later that night, my phone buzzed. *Elliot.*

Hey man. How are things going now that your mom's home?

I stared at the message for a few seconds, thumb hovering over the keyboard.

How *were* things?

We'd made it through dinner without a breakdown. We'd shared memories without falling apart. And even though everything still felt fragile—like one wrong word might shatter it all—it didn't feel as broken as I thought it would.

I finally typed:

It's okay. Different. She's not the mom I remember... but she's getting there.

A few moments passed before his next message came in.

Different good, or different weird?

I smirked a little. Classic Elliot—always cutting through the noise, asking the real question without making it heavy.

Different hopeful, I think, I replied. *Like maybe we've all changed. Not just her.*

There was a pause. Long enough for me to wonder if maybe I'd said too much.

Then—

That might be a good thing, Pat. Change isn't always bad.
Sometimes it's what makes healing possible.
Besides, you're not alone. Not anymore.

That last sentence hit harder than I expected. I blinked at the screen, letting the words settle into the quiet of my room.

He was right. For a long time, I thought I had to carry everything—my grief, my guilt, my silence—alone. But Elliot never let go. Not when I snapped at him. Not when I shut him out. Not even when I'd tried to convince myself I didn't need anyone.

And now, here he was again—still showing up.

I typed back slowly:

Thanks, El. For everything.

A few seconds later:

Always, man. That's what brothers do.

I set my phone down on the nightstand, the soft glow of Elliot's last message still lingering in my mind.

That's what brothers do.

I hadn't had many constants this past year—grief had this way of making everything feel like shifting sand beneath my feet. But somehow, Elliot had stayed solid. A fixed point in the storm.

I sat there a moment longer, the silence of the house settling in around me. It wasn't heavy like before. Just… still.

Then I heard the creak of the floorboards. The soft rustle of a page turning.

I wandered out of my room and found her in the living room, sitting cross-legged on the couch, a thick photo album open on her lap. Her fingers hovered over a picture I knew by heart—Jessi at the lake, mid-laugh, water droplets frozen around her like glitter. Her hair was wild, her nose sunburned, and she looked completely alive.

Mom didn't notice me at first. She just sat there, quiet. Not crying. Not smiling. Just… remembering.

When she finally looked up, her eyes locked on mine. Her voice cracked on my name. "Pat… I owe you an apology."

I shifted, barely shaking my head. "You already did. In the letter."

She closed the album gently and placed her hand on top of it. "No," she said, steady now. "The letter was a start. But this… this needs to come from me. From my mouth. From my heart. You deserve more than ink on a page. You deserve your mom—right here, looking you in the eye—saying she's sorry."

I sat beside her, the couch groaning quietly beneath us.

"I'm sorry I left," she whispered. "Not just when I went to Denver. I left long before that. I disappeared the moment Jessi did. I let the grief swallow me whole, and I drowned myself in wine because I didn't know how to carry the pain. But in trying to numb it, I stopped showing up. For you."

She turned toward me, her voice breaking with something deeper than sadness. "I abandoned you, Patrick. I abandoned my son while he was still bleeding, still trying to make sense of it all. And I will regret that for the rest of my life."

Her hand trembled as she reached for mine. I didn't pull away.

"But I see you now," she said, her eyes glassy. "I see the boy who held this broken family together. I see the strength I didn't have. I see the young man I've missed growing up because I was too lost to look."

I felt the heat rise in my throat. I stared at our hands.

"She had your laugh," Mom whispered, turning her eyes back to the photo of Jessi.

"She had your spirit," I said softly. "Loud. Unfiltered. Kind of impossible not to love."

Mom gave a small, watery chuckle. "I keep thinking about all the moments I missed," she said. "Even before the accident. I was there… but I wasn't *there*. I thought if I kept moving, working, drinking—anything—I wouldn't have to feel what was breaking inside me."

She turned the page. A picture of the four of us on a picnic blanket stared back—Jessi leaning into Dad, me with ketchup on my cheek, Mom mid-laugh, trying to take the photo herself.

"I thought numbing the pain would make it go away," she whispered. "But all it did was make me disappear, too."

The silence settled between us.

"I hated you for a while," I admitted, my voice almost too soft to hear. "Not just for leaving. For shutting down. For not seeing me at all."

She nodded slowly, her eyes cast down. "You had every right to. I was supposed to protect you. I was supposed to be your safe place, and instead… I became part of the hurt."

Then she looked back up, and there was something new in her expression—not shame, not even sadness. Just... honesty. Hope.

"I missed so much," she said gently. "And I know I don't have the right to ask, but… will you tell me about your life now? What I missed while I was gone?"

I hesitated, unsure where to begin.

"Are you still with that girl—Aliza?"

I blinked, surprised she remembered. "Yeah," I said, almost smiling. "We're… figuring things out. She's kind, and honest. And stubborn."

Mom smiled faintly. "Sounds like someone else I know."

I gave her a look. "You, or Jessi?"

She laughed, softer than I remembered, but real. "Take your pick."

Then, after a moment, her tone shifted. More serious. More vulnerable.

"Are you happy, Patrick? Even just a little?"

The question hit deeper than I expected.

"I think… I'm getting there," I said. "I've had some really dark days. But I'm learning how to breathe again. And I'm not alone anymore."

She nodded, her eyes shining. "That's all I could ever want for you."

She looked at me for a long time, like she was trying to memorize the shape of who I'd become. "What else have I missed?" she asked softly. "Tell me everything. Even the boring stuff. I want to know all of it."

So I did.

I told her about Elliot and his terrible jokes. About homecoming and the paint bomb. About Annie's Diner and my red t-shirt, Jessi's favorite. About the dream that haunted me—and the one that helped me start letting go.

She listened to every word like it mattered.

Like *I* mattered.

And for the first time in a long time, I felt like I had a mom again.

Later, when I went back to my room, the house didn't feel hollow. Not the way it had after Jessi died. It felt different—like the walls were starting to remember how to hold warmth again. Like healing didn't come all at once, but in soft, quiet moments when someone decided to stay.

I pulled my blanket up to my chest, fingers brushing the edge of the red tie folded on the nightstand. The one I hadn't been ready for—until I was.

And now… I think I'm ready for this too.

To forgive.

To hope.

To begin again.

Chapter 31 – Kings Who Don't Need Crowns

March arrived without warning—less like a lion or a lamb and more like a shrug. Just… here.

Snow still clung to the sidewalks in gritty patches, stubborn and tired, and the morning air tasted like cold coffee and second chances. School had picked back up after winter break, and with it came the start of third trimester—our last as seniors. The final stretch.

It was strange how quickly things could shift when you weren't waiting for the world to end.

Life at home was… better. Not perfect, but better. Mom had been back for over a month now. Her eyes were clearer, her voice steadier. She cooked dinner a few nights a week, helped clean up without being asked, and even started going to meetings on Tuesdays. Dad joined her sometimes.

They still had moments—fights whispered too loud behind closed doors, or awkward silences during breakfast—but they were *trying*. All of us were. And maybe that's what made it work.

The quiet wasn't so heavy anymore.

Outside of home, the world kept spinning.

Elliot had basically appointed himself my social director. Every weekend, he had a new adventure lined up—a movie night, sledding trip, late-night milkshake run, or "spontaneous character-building experiences," which usually meant getting lost somewhere between here and Denver and pretending it was intentional.

Aliza was part of the crew now, too. She fit in like she'd always belonged—with her teasing smirks, unapologetic honesty, and a habit of slipping her hand into mine when no one else was looking. Erica was with us most weekends, too—sharp-witted, fearless, and louder than all three of us combined. She had a way of turning even the most ordinary hangouts into full-blown events.

The four of us did everything together—late-night fast food runs, impromptu sledding trips, movie marathons where Erica heckled the screen and Elliot insisted on popcorn "theatrics" that usually ended in a mess. It wasn't always smooth, but it was real. And for once, it felt like I belonged.

Sometimes I'd catch myself watching Aliza while she laughed at something Elliot said—head tilted back, eyes shining, like she wasn't carrying the weight of anything—and wonder how I ever thought I could go through this year alone.

I was smitten, plain and simple. Not in the fireworks-and-fairytales kind of way. More like the slow, quiet kind. The kind that catches you when you least expect it and makes the world feel a little less heavy.

And every time her fingers found mine, I held on like I wasn't ready to let go.

It was Monday morning when I heard the rumor.

First day of the final trimester.

I was at my locker, wrestling with a jammed zipper on my backpack, when I heard two underclassmen whispering behind me.

"...yeah, he's back. Saw him in the office this morning getting his schedule."

"No way. I thought he dropped out."

"His parents homeschooled him after the paint thing. But I guess he's finishing out the year here. Walking with the class and everything."

The zipper gave way with a snap, and I was the one now stuck.

David Bell.

Back at Black Hills.

For a second, the air around me shifted—tightened, like an old wound remembering what it felt like to bleed. My breath caught. The hallway around me blurred. It was like no time had passed at all.

The old feelings crept in, silent and sharp—the shrinking in my chest, the way my shoulders curved inward without permission. I could already hear his voice—sarcastic, biting. Feel the sting of his laughter echoing down the halls.

And just like that, I was back at square one. The punchline again. The ghost.

I slammed my locker shut, hands trembling.

Maybe I wasn't as far along as I thought.

By lunch, the buzz had settled into a low hum across campus. Whispers followed me from one class to the next.

"Did you hear David's back?"

"Wonder what he's gonna say to Schwartz."

"I bet this year just got a whole lot more interesting…"

I didn't want interesting. I wanted peace.

The nerves returned when I stepped into the cafeteria—old instincts telling me to keep my head down, find a corner, don't make eye contact.

But then I looked across the room.

Elliot was waving, mouth full of pizza. Erica sat next to him, animatedly reenacting some dramatic story with her hands, and Aliza leaned into her side, laughing so hard she nearly spilled her soda.

And there was a seat saved just for me.

My chest loosened.

I wasn't alone.

Not this time.

Not anymore.

I walked toward them—past stares, past whispers, past the shadows of who I used to be—and slid into the seat like I belonged there.

Because I did.

I'd barely unwrapped my sandwich when the energy in the cafeteria shifted.

It started with the hush. A ripple of voices tapering off. Then the shuffling. Heads turning. Forks pausing mid-air.

And then, like a scene from a bad teen movie, **David Bell** strutted through the double doors.

Same smug grin. Same athlete's gait like the floor owed him a favor. But something was different now. Maybe it was the lack of a letterman jacket. Or the fact that his usual entourage wasn't trailing behind him. Maybe it was just me.

He scanned the room like he expected applause.

He didn't get it.

A few freshmen leaned in to whisper. Someone near the soda machine muttered, "Is that really him?"

David walked with purpose, straight toward our table, his smile widening with every step.

My heart thumped once—hard—then settled. I sat still, eyes forward, like I wasn't fazed. Even if part of me was.

"Schwartz," he said, stopping right behind me. "Man… long time."

Elliot sat up straighter. Erica rolled her eyes so hard I thought they might get stuck.

Aliza didn't move. But her grip tightened around my hand.

I turned slowly in my seat, meeting David's eyes. His smile didn't reach his.

"Didn't think you'd still be here," he added. "After everything."

"Yeah?" I said. "Well… here I am."

He chuckled, low and mocking. "Guess you really milked that Homecoming crown, huh? Paint and pity—great combo."

I felt the tension around me spike.

And then—

"Back off, Bell," Erica said, standing up slightly. "You don't get to walk in here like nothing happened."

David blinked. "Excuse me?"

"You heard her," Elliot said, his voice calm but firm. "No one missed you."

A few tables over, someone muttered, *"Jerk."*

Another voice: *"Thought he transferred."*

David's smile twitched. "Wow. Guess I was gone longer than I thought. Tables really turned around here, huh?"

I stood up slowly, not because I felt threatened—but because I didn't want to give him the illusion that he could stand over me.

"You came back looking for something, David," I said. "But the thing is… no one's giving it to you."

He tilted his head. "What's that?"

"Attention," I said simply. "The power. The control. All that noise you used to live for? It doesn't work anymore. Not here. Not with me."

David stared at me, like he didn't recognize the person in front of him.

Maybe he didn't.

Because I wasn't afraid of him anymore.

He scoffed. "Whatever, man."

And just like that, he turned and walked off—no insults, no comeback, no applause.

Just silence.

And then… a few claps.

Not loud or dramatic.

Just enough.

Enough to say: We saw that. We're with you.

I sat down again, heart pounding—but not from fear.

From something else.

Elliot grinned. "Legend."

Erica raised her soda. "To kings who don't need crowns."

Aliza leaned over, her voice soft but full of pride. "You were incredible."

I took a deep breath, looked around the room—and for the first time in forever, I felt seen not as the boy who broke, but the boy who *stood back up.*

That night, after dinner and a quiet hour pretending to do homework, I pulled the journal Aliza gave me from my desk drawer.

The leather was soft and worn at the edges, the ribbon bookmark tucked neatly between two pages I hadn't touched yet. On the inside cover, her handwriting still made me smile—

"For the words you haven't said yet. I hope they find you."

I flipped to the next blank page. A prompt was written across the top in her looping cursive:

"Write about the moment you realized you weren't the same person you were at the beginning of the year."

I stared at the sentence for a long time. Let the weight of it settle.

Then I picked up my pen.

March 4th

I used to think strength meant being loud—being the one who walked into a room and made people shrink back. I used to think pain was something you had to bury, or else it would bury you.
That if you hurt long enough, deep enough, you'd just… vanish. And maybe that was easier.

But today, David Bell—the guy who once made me feel like nothing—looked at me like *he* was the one disappearing.
And I didn't yell. I didn't fight.
I just stood there, steady. Quiet. Whole.

And I didn't flinch.

Not because I'm fearless.
But because I'm not the same boy I was in September.

I'm not just the kid who lost his sister.
Not the one dripping in paint and shame.
Not the boy begging the world to see him.

I'm still grieving. Still healing. Still figuring out who I am.
But today, I stood tall.
Not in anger. Not in revenge.
Just… in truth.

And maybe that's what strength really is.

Not crowns. Not titles. Not noise.
Just the choice to stay standing—especially when it would be easier to run.

I set the pen down and closed the journal softly, the warmth of Aliza's words still lingering like a hand on my shoulder.

And for the first time in a long time, I didn't feel like I needed to win anything.

Because I'd already won something better.

Chapter 32 – Firelight and Futures

The fire crackled softly, casting long shadows across the patio as we passed around a bag of marshmallows and a half-empty bottle of root beer. The only light came from the flicker of the flames and a couple of dim windows glowing from inside Aliza's house. The air smelled like smoke and melted sugar, and a quiet playlist hummed behind us—something indie, something nostalgic.

We'd spent the last few hours laughing about dumb middle school memories and near-death experiences in Elliot's old Jeep. But now the energy had shifted—like we all felt it, hovering just under the surface.

Time was running out.

"I did the math," Erica said, leaning back in her camping chair with a marshmallow on fire. "We've got like... six weeks left. Then it's over."

"Thanks for that, Grim Reaper," Elliot muttered, tossing a pebble toward her.

She shrugged, grinning. "Hey, someone had to say it."

A beat of silence.

Then Elliot exhaled and broke it. "So... is this the part where we all share our college plans like a Netflix original?"

We all laughed, but the truth settled in anyway. This was happening. Soon.

Erica went first.

"I committed to Colorado State on a soccer scholarship," she said casually, like it wasn't a big deal. "Gonna major in psych. Or criminal justice. Or... something that lets me boss people around."

"You do that already," I said.

She pointed at me with her marshmallow stick. "Exactly. Why mess with perfection?"

We laughed, but there was pride in her voice, too. And she deserved it.

Elliot nudged her with his shoulder. "I'll be crashing her vibe at Colorado State."

"You got in?" I asked, my eyes lighting up.

"Yep," he said, a little sheepish. "Business major. I mean, unless I tank econ next tri. But yeah. CSU."

"Dude, that's awesome." I meant it. Seeing him light up like that—it was rare. And it felt good.

Erica raised her soda. "Here's to dorm snacks and questionable decisions."

"I'll be there to rescue you from dumb ideas," she added, deadpan.

Then it was my turn.

"I'm going to Colorado," I said. "Not CSU—just outside Denver. Small school. I want to be a Child Life Specialist."

Aliza looked at me, her eyes softening. "That's perfect for you."

I shrugged. "Figured if I can make it through this year, maybe I can help someone else survive theirs."

No one said anything for a moment. Then Elliot nodded slowly.

"That's... really cool, man."

"Thanks," I said. "Still scares me a little."

"Good," Erica said. "Means it matters."

Then, everyone looked at Aliza.

She smiled. But it didn't quite reach her eyes.

"I accepted a cheer scholarship to UCLA," she said, brushing ash off her jeans. "It's full ride. And they have a great nursing program."

"Whoa," Erica said. "That's amazing."

"Yeah," Elliot echoed. "Like, sunshine and palm trees and celebrities. You'll fit right in."

Aliza laughed softly. "And traffic and overpriced smoothies and... I don't know. Maybe it'll be good."

I watched her as she spoke—how her voice rose a little too high at the end of her sentences, how her fingers twisted the bracelet on her wrist. She talked about all the things we could do when I visited her in the fall—hiking in the hills, catching a game at the Rose Bowl, crashing a studio tour like tourists.

I smiled. I congratulated her. I told her how proud I was.

But something in my chest tightened.

Not because I wasn't happy for her—I was. More than I could say.

But buried underneath the pride was a fear I couldn't shake.
A fear that this—this firelight, this closeness, this *us*—was only temporary.
That no matter how strong the bond, time and distance would stretch it thin until one day it just… snapped.
That Aliza would go to UCLA, build a life full of new people, new dreams, and maybe—just maybe—forget the boy who never thought he'd survive senior year.

And the worst part?

I wasn't sure I could blame her.

The conversation quieted as the fire settled into glowing embers, crackling softly beneath a sky freckled with stars. Aliza leaned her head against my shoulder. Erica was poking at the coals with a stick, and Elliot stared into the flames like he was watching something only he could see.

Then, without a word, he stood up and grabbed a half-full soda can from the ground.

"I'm not good at stuff like this," he started, eyes still on the fire. "But I feel like... this kind of night deserves a moment."

We all looked up at him, waiting.

He cleared his throat.

"A year ago, I don't think any of us could've pictured this—*us*—right here. We've all been through stuff. Some of it loud, some of it silent. But we made it through."

The firelight danced across his face as he looked at each of us.

"To Erica," he said, raising the can, "for always speaking her mind, even when no one asked—and somehow being right more often than not."

Erica smirked but didn't interrupt. Her eyes shimmered, just a little.

"To Aliza—for showing up when it mattered most, for seeing things in people even when they couldn't see it in themselves... and for making him" —he nodded toward me— "believe in good things again."

Aliza squeezed my hand.

Elliot turned to me last.

"And to Patrick. For standing back up. For choosing to keep going. For proving that strength doesn't have to be loud to be real."

My throat tightened, but I stayed quiet.

Elliot looked down at his can, then back at all of us.

"To lifelong friendship," he said, voice steady. "To the people we used to be, and the people we're still becoming. And to the road ahead—wherever it takes us."

He raised his can.

We clinked whatever we had—metal, plastic, marshmallow sticks—and let the silence fill in what words couldn't.

The kind of silence that didn't feel empty.

The kind that felt like *everything.*

The fire had settled into its final glow, the embers pulsing faintly beneath a blanket of ash. The playlist had long stopped. Even the stars above seemed quieter somehow, like they were giving us a little extra time before the night was truly over.

Elliot had one arm wrapped around Erica, her head resting on his shoulder as they watched the fire fade. Aliza leaned into me, her cheek brushing the side of my neck. I pulled her closer, my arm curled around her back, and we sat in silence—two pairs of souls suspended in a moment that already felt like a memory.

The crackle of burning wood gave way to stillness. Just the rhythmic breath of the people I loved and the slow dimming of the flames.

Elliot stood first, stretching with a low groan.

"I'm calling it," he said, brushing soot off his jeans. "Gotta pretend to be responsible in the morning."

Erica stood up with him and tossed her marshmallow stick into the ashes. "Try not to forget your Econ homework *again,* future businessman."

He shot her a look, but she just grinned.

Then Elliot turned to me and opened his arms like it was an inside joke. "Get over here, you emotionally evolved marshmallow."

I rolled my eyes, but stood up and wrapped him in a hug anyway. A solid, real one—the kind that says *thank you* and *I've got you* without needing the words.

"I'll see you tomorrow," he said, pulling back.

"Yeah," I replied. "Thanks for… all of it."

He just nodded. Then he and Erica headed off toward his car, their laughter trailing behind them like the last note of a favorite song.

I sat back down beside Aliza. The last of the warmth lingered between us, and in the soft, fading glow from the coals, her eyes still looked like they held something ancient—something quietly burning, even after the fire was gone.

"I'm proud of you," I said softly.

She looked over, a little surprised.

"I mean it," I added. "UCLA's lucky to have you."

She smiled, but it was quieter this time. "Thanks, Patch."

I stared at the fire for a second before finding the courage to finish what I needed to say.

"I don't ever want to be the reason something doesn't happen for you," I said. "I want you to chase what you love. Full speed. No looking back."

She didn't respond right away. She just reached for my hand, intertwining our fingers in the space between us.

"Okay," she whispered.

Then, slowly, she leaned in and pressed her lips to mine—soft, warm, unhurried.
Like a thank you.
Like a promise.
Like she heard everything I said… and everything I didn't.

When she pulled back, she didn’t say anything.

She didn’t have to.

Chapter 33 – It Felt Like Remembering

I didn't expect it to feel like this.

Standing at the bottom of the basement stairs, duffel bag in one hand, laundry basket in the other, I looked around one last time.

The room I had turned into a cave.
Where the shadows felt safer than sunlight.
Where I could scream without anyone hearing and sleep without the sound of her laugh seeping through the walls.

It was my refuge.
My prison.
My in-between.

And now, I was done hiding in it.

It didn't happen all at once. Healing never does. But today, for the first time in a long time, I didn't feel trapped here.

I felt ready.

So I packed. The books I still loved. The worn hoodie I clung to for months. The half-finished drawings I never showed anyone.

I left the broken headphones on the desk. The blanket that still smelled like fear.

Some things don't need to come upstairs.

When I finally climbed the steps and opened the door to my old room, it felt strange—but not bad. Like stepping into a memory that doesn't hurt the way it used to.

The walls were still blue. The dresser still squeaked. But the air felt different now.

It was still quiet. But not the kind that presses on your chest. This quiet came with open windows, soft laughter, and the smell of dinner on the stove.

It lived in the little things: the way Mom hummed sometimes while she cooked. The way Dad actually came into the kitchen to ask about her day. The way we remembered to say goodnight—and meant it. Sometimes, we even said I love you, and no one flinched.

Spring had started to arrive in Colorado, slow and stubborn. Snow still lined the curbs, but the sun hung a little longer each evening. Patches of brown grass were finally winning their fight to breathe.

It had been months since Mom came home from Denver. And somehow, through the awkward dinners and quiet mornings, the tension had started to fade. Not vanish. Just… loosen its grip.

One Saturday morning, I stood at the top of the stairs and looked down the hallway—past the linen closet, past the bathroom, to the room we didn't talk about.

Jessi's room.

The door was barely cracked—not out of remembrance, but avoidance. Like none of us wanted to see what was left behind.

Later that afternoon, over grilled cheese sandwiches and chips, I looked at Mom and Dad and said the words before I could second-guess them.

"What if we cleaned out Jessi's room?"

They both froze. Mom's hand paused on her glass. Dad looked up like I'd said something in a language none of us had spoken in a long time.

"I don't mean—like, erasing her," I added quickly. "Just… fixing it. Together. Making it hers again."

The silence stretched.

Then Mom nodded. Slowly. "Yeah," she said. "Yeah. I think… it's time."

Dad didn't say anything at first. Just stared at his plate.

Then finally: "Okay."

We started the next morning.

I opened the door like I was visiting someone who'd moved out without packing.

The room was still frozen in that awful moment—books knocked off shelves, drawers half-open, her mirror cracked along one edge. The rug bunched up like someone had tripped. Shards of broken ceramic peeked out from beneath the dresser—what remained of her little jewelry tray.

One picture frame lay face-down near the window. A few books scattered on the floor. The corner of the desk scuffed like something had been thrown.

The bedspread was rumpled, half-hanging off the mattress, like someone had yanked it and never bothered to fix it.

The room felt unsettled—like it had absorbed everything we never said and held onto it. Quietly. Patiently. Waiting.

Nothing had been touched since.

Not really.

But her fingerprints were everywhere.
Photos on the wall. Glittery pens in a chipped mason jar. A faded poster of her favorite band. Her hoodie, still draped over the chair like she'd just taken it off.

Mom stood in the doorway and let out a shaky breath.

"We'll take it slow," she whispered.

We didn't talk much at first.

We just worked.

Mom sorted clothes into donation bags. Dad quietly screwed the closet door back onto its hinges. I stacked books and folded blankets. The silence wasn't awkward—it was full. Full of her.

It wasn't long before the memories came.

"Remember when she used to rearrange her whole room every two weeks?" Mom said, holding up a crooked lamp.

"She said it kept the energy fresh," I added.

Dad chuckled. "She moved the bed once at two in the morning. Woke up the whole house."

"And then blamed it on the cat," I said, smiling.

Mom shook her head, wiping tears with the back of her hand. "Goodness, she was impossible."

"But in the best way," I said.

A few hours later, we'd made progress.

The room looked lived in again. Lighter. Like it could breathe.

We sat on the floor together, leaning against the bed frame. A pile of old photos lay scattered between us—Jessi in Halloween costumes, on vacation, in goofy selfies none of us remembered taking.

Dad picked up one—Jessi, mid-laugh, frosting on her nose. He smiled, and this time, it didn't look like it hurt.

"I think she'd like this," he said quietly. "Us. Together."

And for once, I didn't feel like we were breaking.

I felt like we were beginning again.

After we finished Jessi's room, something shifted in our house.

Not in a loud, obvious way. But in the quiet comfort of shared meals. Unlocked doors. Sunlight that didn't feel heavy when it came through the windows.

There were still hard days. Grief didn't leave.

But it didn't run the place anymore.

By the time May rolled around, we were talking about graduation, college, and prom like people who believed in the future again.

And for the first time…

So did I.

Chapter 34 – Where the Hurt Ends

Prom wasn't supposed to matter. Not to me.

At the start of the year, I told myself I wouldn't go. That it was just another dance. Another night of pretending to belong in a world that didn't want me.

But things change.

People change.

And somehow, here I was—standing in front of the mirror in a button-down shirt and tie, straightening my jacket with a quiet kind of calm. The kind that comes when you've already faced the worst, and somehow... you're still here.

I didn't feel anxious. Or invisible. Or broken.

I felt ready.

The doorbell rang at exactly five.

I heard Elliot's voice through the screen door before I even made it downstairs.

"Let's go, fashionably on time!"

I laughed under my breath and grabbed my jacket from the hook.

Dad was in the kitchen, holding his phone like he wanted to take a picture but wasn't sure if he should. "You look good, Pat."

"Thanks," I said, surprised by how much that meant.

He gave me a nod—the quiet kind, like we both understood how far this moment had come from where we started.

Then I stepped outside into the golden light of early evening.

Elliot stood at the curb in a pressed shirt, jacket half-buttoned, hair doing its own thing. Erica leaned against the car, arms crossed, smirking as she looked me up and down.

"Not bad, Schwartz," she said. "Didn't expect you to clean up this well."

"Didn't expect you to wear heels," I shot back.

"They're combat heels. Stylish and dangerous."

Elliot gave me a playful elbow. "C'mon. Let's go pick up your girl."

I smiled at the phrase—*your girl.* Still felt unreal.

Aliza's house looked like a postcard. There were flowers blooming on the porch and light spilling through the front windows. She stepped outside just as we pulled up.

And everything stopped.

She wore a midnight blue dress that fell just above her knees—simple, stunning, effortless. Her hair was half-up, softly curled, like the wind itself had shaped it. And when her eyes found mine, she smiled and crinkled her nose like the world had narrowed down to this one moment.

"Hey," I said, as she approached.

"Hey," she whispered back, slipping her hand into mine.

"Wow," Erica muttered from behind us. "Should've brought tissues."

We took pictures in front of the car—silly ones, serious ones, one where Elliot pretended to propose to Erica and she mock-ran down the driveway. Aliza and I took one just the two of us, and I couldn't stop smiling. Not because I had to. But because I wanted to.

Afterward, we headed straight to the bowling alley on the edge of town—the old-school one with black lights, neon shoes, and a jukebox that only played music from before we were born.

It was ridiculous. And perfect.

We walked in like we owned the place—or at least like we'd lost a bet. Elliot was already swapping his dress shoes for a pair of bowling ones two sizes too big, and Erica was spinning her "combat heels" like she was about to launch them into orbit. Aliza lifted the hem of her midnight blue dress just enough to walk with exaggerated elegance, and I followed behind her like this was the best pre-prom decision we'd ever made.

Erica bowled a strike on her first try and demanded we replay the moment in slow motion with dramatic commentary. Elliot tried to match her and immediately slipped. I barely kept my ball out of the gutter.

And Aliza?

She nudged me after another strike. "So… you're just here for moral support, right?"

"Exactly," I said. "Gotta let someone else shine tonight."

She smirked. "I'm flattered. But don't think I'm going easy on you at the dance."

By the time we arrived at prom, the sun had dipped below the horizon and the sky glowed with that in-between color—soft blue giving way to silver. The school gym had been transformed, at least as much as a gym *can* be transformed. There were white string lights looping across the rafters, gold and silver streamers hanging from the ceiling, and round tables pushed to the sides with half-melted candles flickering in glass jars.

A slow song played over the speakers as we walked in.

And this time, nobody stared.

Nobody whispered.

No one looked at me like I didn't belong.

We were just… there. Together. Four seniors in formal wear, laughing and loud, dancing offbeat and on purpose.

I'd spent so much of the year surviving moments like this. Now I was living one.

Elliot and Erica danced like no one was watching—but with just enough coordination to make it look effortless. He spun her during the fast songs, held her close during the slow ones. The kind of dancing that wasn't about showing off—it was about enjoying the moment.

Aliza pulled me onto the dance floor, her fingers laced with mine as the lights spun in gold and blue. Around us, classmates moved like shadows in the shimmer, laughter blending with music that felt a little too loud but not in a bad way. The gym smelled faintly of cheap cologne, punch, and something sweet—like hope or maybe nostalgia.

The lights dimmed just slightly, and the tempo slowed.

A new song floated through the speakers—low and warm, like something pulled from a dusty vinyl record:

"I would never fall in love again… until I found you…"

I felt Aliza's hand slip into mine.

She didn't say anything—just guided me to the center of the floor like it was the most natural thing in the world.

Her arms draped over my shoulders. Mine found their way to her waist.

We moved slowly, swaying in time with the music, the rest of the world blurring around us. There were no phones. No whispers. Just the two of us and a song that sounded a little too close to the truth.

She rested her head against my chest.

And I knew—right there, right then—that I needed to say it.

Not because I had to.

But because it was real.

I leaned in, my lips brushing just beside her ear.

"I love you," I whispered.

She didn't freeze. Didn't pull away.

Instead, she lifted her head to meet my eyes.

Her expression was soft. Steady.

"I know," she said, her voice soft but steady. Her eyes didn't leave mine. "You didn't have to say it tonight. You didn't owe me anything. But I'm really glad you did."

She leaned in just a little closer, her forehead almost touching mine.

"Because I love you too, Patrick."

We didn't say anything for a while after that.

We just swayed, the song wrapping around us like a promise. I held her a little tighter, and she didn't let go.

When the music ended, we didn't rush to leave. None of us did.

Eventually, the lights came up, and the last song played. People started heading home, fixing their hair, looking for lost phones, hugging classmates they'd never speak to again.

We found Elliot and Erica sitting outside on the curb, Erica barefoot, her heels in one hand and a melted slushie in the other. Elliot leaned back on his hands, looking up at the sky like he didn't want the night to end.

Aliza and I sat beside them, our arms brushing, legs stretched out onto the pavement still holding the warmth of the day.

No one said much.

We didn't need to.

We'd laughed. We'd danced. We'd survived.

And now we were just here.

Four seniors.
A spring night.
A quiet goodbye to everything that used to hurt.

I looked around at them—all of them—and for the first time, I wasn't trying to catch up to someone else's life or outrun my own.

I was just here.
In this moment.
And I was happy.

Chapter 35 –The Weight of Words

I wake up to my alarm.

It's time to get ready.

The long-awaited day—Graduation Day.

This will be my last day of high school. I honestly can't believe how fast it's gone. The year didn't just slip by—it flew. And somehow, here I am.

As I sit up in bed, I start to reflect. Not just on the school year, but on everything that came before it. Everything that brought me here.

I'm not the same person I was almost a year ago, after I lost Jessi.
Honestly? I'm not even the same person I was with Jessi.

I'm happier now than I've ever been.

And I don't think I would've made it here on my own.

The guilt, the grief, the loneliness—it could've eaten me alive. But I didn't let it. Or maybe... I didn't let it *win.* Because I finally chose to open my heart. I stopped pretending I was fine. I admitted I needed help. And when I did, the right people showed up.

The first person I think of is Elliot—my best friend. My brother in every way that counts.

We've been through it together. I helped him grieve when he lost his parents in elementary school. This year, he returned the favor. He stood beside me when I couldn't stand on my own. He made me laugh when I didn't think I ever would again. He reminded me that sometimes, we survive the hard things because someone else holds us up.

Then there's Aliza.

In August, I barely knew her. I never imagined we'd become friends—let alone... whatever we are now. But she saw through the walls I put up. She didn't walk away when things got messy. She leaned in.

She's the Valedictorian. Of course she is. She got into UCLA, USC, UNLV, and probably every other college that starts with a vowel. She's heading to UCLA in the fall on a full-ride scholarship—and she'll be cheering for them on Saturdays.

I should feel sad. I should feel afraid of losing all this—of losing her.

But right now? I just feel proud. Of her. Of Elliot. And maybe—just maybe—of myself.

I got up and started getting ready—shower, teeth, the usual routine. But everything felt different today. Lighter. Like the weight I used to carry had finally loosened its grip on my chest.

I pulled open my dresser drawer and dug out my favorite jeans—worn, faded, probably not graduation-appropriate, but completely *me*. Then I reached for the red shirt.

Jessi's favorite.

It still smelled faintly like that old detergent she loved. I used to hate wearing it because it reminded me of her. Today, I put it on because it does.

It felt right—like she'd be with me when I walked that stage.

Just as I threw it on, I heard the front door open and Aliza's voice float through the house.

"Patrick?" she called. "You better not be going to graduation in those jeans."

I smiled and came downstairs, and there she was—standing in the living room in a white summer dress with a tiny black box in her hands.

She looked me up and down, a smirk tugging at her lips. "*The jeans. Of course.*"

"What can I say?" I shrugged. "It's a signature look."

"I knew you'd wear them," she said, stepping closer. "You're nothing if not predictable."

"Comfortable," I corrected.

She rolled her eyes. "Predictably comfortable."

Then she held out the box. "Okay, Mr. Denim—this is for you. Graduation morning tradition. I decided that's a thing."

I took it from her, carefully untied the ribbon, and lifted the lid.

Inside was a soft, pale blue button-down shirt—simple, clean, brand new.

"I figured you could wear that over the red shirt," she said, her voice soft. "That way Jessi's with you. But so are we."

For a second, I couldn't speak. I just looked at her, this girl who somehow knew exactly what I needed before I did.

"Thank you," I said, my voice catching just slightly.

She reached for my hand and gave it a small squeeze. "You ready?"

I threw on my new shirt.

I nodded. "Let's do this."

Most of the morning is filled with busy work—cleaning out desks, organizing old portfolios, returning books we barely opened, and pretending to care about surveys we'll never look at again. The teachers are more checked out than we are. Some play movies. Others just sit at their desks, sipping coffee and letting the hours slip by.

We pass the time the only way we know how—talking, signing yearbooks, looping back through old memories like we're flipping through a photo album that's still being written.

We laugh at the awkward moments, the inside jokes, the teachers we swore hated us.
We tease each other about freshman year haircuts and bad cafeteria food.
We talk about what's next, and what we wish we'd done differently.

Some of us cry—quietly, or not so quietly.

Because even though we've spent the last four years waiting to get out of this place, something about it still matters. Something about these cracked floors and scuffed lockers and familiar hallways feels like home, even if we never said it out loud.

We know it won't ever be like this again.

As much as we've all complained about Black Hills, we know deep down… this is it.

Some of us won't see each other again. Not at graduation. Not ever. Even best friends—like Elliot—won't be at your side every day anymore. Maybe not even every week.

That's what I think I'll miss most. The closeness. The rhythm of *us*.

The rest of the morning is yearbooks and selfies and people promising to "stay in touch" even though most won't.

When the lunch bell rings, I meet up with Aliza and our usual group. She packed a lunch, like always. We settle in, trading chips and inside jokes, when a voice interrupts the table.

"Do you mind if I sit with you?"

We all look up, unsure who's asking.
And I nearly fall off the bench when I see it's David.

I freeze. But before I can speak, Aliza does.

"We'd rather you not," she says, firm but not cruel. "No offense, but you've bullied and betrayed every one of us. Today's supposed to be special… and we don't want it ruined."

David nods. "I understand. I don't blame you."

He starts to walk away, tray in hand. But something makes me get up and follow.

"Hey—" I call out.

He turns, eyes wary.

"Why our table?" I ask. "Why now?"

The cafeteria gets quiet. Too quiet.

David sets his tray on a random table. "You don't get it, do you?"

I stare, confused. Bracing.

"I had it all," he says. "A full-ride scholarship. A roadmap to the NFL. A girlfriend. Popularity. Power. And now?" He shrugs. "I've got nothing. I lost it all."

He stops. For a second, I'm not sure if he's about to punch me or break down.

"I wanted to sit with you to apologize," he continues. "Because this is our last day of high school. And I know I may never be on top again. Not like I was here."

He swallows hard.

"I made your life miserable. And others', too. I don't expect forgiveness. But I needed to say it—Patrick, I'm sorry. For everything."

Then he walks out of the cafeteria. Quiet. Alone.

I turn back to our table. Everyone's jaws are basically on the floor. I sit down, stunned.

I walked back to the table like I was underwater—everything muffled, every step slow. No one said a word. Not even Elliot.

I sat down and stared at my tray, unsure whether to feel vindicated… or just sad.

We grab our stuff and head to the auditorium.

On the way, I glance at Aliza. "What just happened? Am I supposed to feel… guilty now?"

She stops walking and turns to me, her hand resting gently on my cheek.

"Patrick, no. None of this is your fault. David was cruel. He made choices. And now he's living with the consequences. That's on him—not you."

We sit with Elliot and Erica near the middle row—our group. Our people. It's nice, having them.

The assembly flies by. A few songs. A couple skits. A slideshow of baby pictures and awkward middle school smiles. Laughter echoes. A few tears are shed. Teachers wave from the side like we're heading off to space.

At the end, we're reminded to be back by 5:00. Caps, gowns, tassels—ready to walk by 6:00 sharp.

The clock is ticking.

And for once, I'm not afraid.

As the assembly ends and the crowd starts to thin, Aliza and I head for the exits with the rest of the senior class. We're almost to the hallway when we hear our names called out over the chatter.

"Patrick. Aliza."

We turn.
It's Principal Powell, waving us over from the front of the auditorium.

"Do you have just a minute?" he asks, his voice warm. "Both of you."

"Sure," we say at the same time.

We follow him down the hall to his office. He holds the door open for us, then gestures toward the two chairs in front of his desk. "Have a seat."

Aliza crosses her legs and folds her hands in her lap. I sit a little stiffly, unsure what this is about.

"Aliza," he begins, "are you ready for your speech tonight? You've earned this moment. I know how hard you've worked."

She nods, nerves dancing in her smile. "Almost. I have a few last-minute edits to make, but I'll get there. I've never spoken in front of this many people before."

"You'll do great," he says. "This town's like family. They're proud of you. Just like I am."

He turns to me next, and something shifts in his eyes—gentler. He hesitates before speaking, like he's trying to find the right words.

"Patrick…" he begins, his voice steady but low. "I just want you to know how proud I am of you."

He shifts in his seat, folding his hands in front of him.

"After the accident… and everything that followed… most students would've shut down. And when Homecoming happened—I'll be honest, I wasn't sure you'd come back at all. But you did."

He pauses, eyes beginning to glisten.

"You came back. You faced it. And you didn't just survive this year, Patrick—you changed. You grew into someone thoughtful, someone resilient. Someone who's quietly made this school a better place by choosing not to give up."

He exhales, and his voice softens.

"I'm sorry. For everything you've had to carry. For what happened that night, and for what it took you to make it here. You deserved better support. And I don't know if anyone's told you this yet, but... you've made a lot of people proud. Me included."

The room falls quiet.

My chest tightens. My eyes sting.

"Thank you, sir," I manage to say, my voice catching.

He nods once—like the kind of nod that says *I mean it*—then leans back slightly in his chair.

Principal Powell clears his throat, then leans forward slightly, resting his elbows on the desk.

"I'd like to ask you something, Patrick," he says, his tone more serious now. "Something important."

I nod, unsure where this is going.

"I'd like you to give the closing remarks tonight at commencement."

I blink.

"Instead of me," he adds, with a small smile.

I stare at him, completely thrown.

"You've experienced more than most of your classmates," he continues. "And you've done something with it. You've grown. You've healed. You've helped others heal just by showing up, day after day. You've lived through the hardest parts of being human, and you've come out of it wiser—more grounded."

He lets the words settle in the room.

"I think you have something real to say. Something this class—this community—needs to hear. And I can't think of anyone better to deliver it."

My mouth opens, but nothing comes out.
I'm not sure if I'm supposed to say thank you or run.

Me? Give a speech? On graduation night? In front of everyone?

"I—" I finally stammer.

But Aliza squeezes my hand and cuts in gently.

"He'd be honored," she says, smiling.

I glance at her, and she nods like *you've got this.*

Principal Powell stands. "Good. I knew I could count on you."

He walks us to the door and pauses just before opening it.

"Keep it to about ten minutes," he adds. "Speak from the heart. That's what people will remember."

Then he opens the door and gives each of us a small, proud nod.

"Congratulations to you both. I'll see you at five."

Chapter 36 – Something Worth Saying

We leave Principal Powell's office, and I still haven't fully processed what just happened. I'm going to speak at graduation. In front of the entire senior class. Their families. The whole town.

"Me?" I finally whisper as we step outside into the bright afternoon sun.

"Yes, you," Aliza says, bumping her shoulder against mine. "You've got this."

I shake my head. "I don't even have a speech. I don't even have a shirt that doesn't have some kind of ketchup stain on it."

She grins. "Then we've got work to do."

We run to my house first so I can change into something more formal. Aliza waits on the couch while I dig through my closet like I'm on a timed game show. Eventually, I settle on slacks, a navy tie, and the canary yellow button-down shirt she had given to me for Christmas, with the journal. The one I wasn't ready to embrace.

When I come downstairs, she gives me a quick nod of approval.

"Acceptable," she says. "Not bad for a guy who was ready to wear jeans to graduation."

"Comfort is a lifestyle."

"Public speaking is not," she replies. "Let's go. You've got a speech to write."

We drive to her house and head straight upstairs. She sits at her desk and pulls up her speech draft, fingers tapping anxiously against the keys. I pace behind her, chewing on my thumbnail and mentally running through every possible way to fail in front of a thousand people.

After a minute, she swivels in her chair to face me.

"Okay," she says. "I need a second set of eyes. Want to hear it?"

I nod and sit on the edge of her bed, legs bouncing.

She takes a breath, then starts reading. Her voice is clear but careful, like she's still shaping the words as she says them. It's good. Thoughtful. Honest. Aliza kind of speech.

But about halfway through, she stumbles on a transition.

"Wait," I say, holding up a hand. "Right there—between the story about the library volunteer trip and your advice to underclassmen—it's a little… jumpy."

She re-reads it, frowning. "You're right. It needs a bridge."

"What if you added something like, 'There were moments we thought we'd never make it—but we did. And not alone.' Or something like that?"

Her eyes light up. She turns back to the screen and types.

"You're kind of good at this," she says.

"I'm kind of panicking about writing mine," I reply.

She finishes editing her draft and hits save, then spins her chair back toward me.

"Okay," she says. "Your turn."

I freeze. "You're staying right?"

"Of course I'm staying," she says, reaching for my hand. "You helped me. I'm helping you. That's what we do."

I sit at her computer and stare at the blinking cursor.

Nothing comes out.

I scroll through a few Google Docs for inspiration, then immediately feel like a fraud. None of it sounds like me. Too polished. Too rehearsed. Too… not real.

"How do I even start this?" I ask, glancing at Aliza. "I don't want it to sound like a cliché."

She doesn't hesitate. "Be honest. Be yourself."

I look at her. She means it. Every word.

I nod slowly and turn back to the screen.
Be honest. Be myself.

I take a deep breath.
And I begin typing.

The words come slowly at first, like they're unsure if they belong. But then—like they've been waiting inside me all year—they start to flow. I don't overthink it. I don't try to sound impressive. I just write what's true.

About Jessi.
About Elliot.
About Aliza.
About guilt, healing, choices.

Aliza stays quiet beside me, reading over my shoulder, nodding now and then but never interrupting.

It's the first time in a long time I've felt peace while putting my story into words.

When I finish, I lean back and stare at the screen.

"I think… I think I'm done," I say, surprised.

Aliza scans the final paragraph, then looks up at me with tears in her eyes.

I don't say anything at first. Neither does she.

The hum of her laptop is the only sound between us, but it doesn't feel awkward. It feels… full. Like the silence is holding something important.

I glance at her.

She's still looking at the screen, but not reading anymore. Just sitting with it. With me.

"Does it make sense?" I ask quietly. "Like, does it feel too heavy or too… I don't know, raw?"

She turns to face me fully.

"It feels real," she says. "And brave. And maybe yeah, it's raw—but that's why it's perfect. Because it's *you*. And people need to hear it."

I look down at my hands.

"I didn't think I could do this," I admit. "Not just the speech. All of it. This year."

Her hand finds mine and squeezes.

"You didn't do it alone."

I nod. My throat tightens.

"I think Jessi would've liked it," I say, almost to myself.

Aliza leans her head against my shoulder.

"She would've been the first one on her feet."

We sit there like that for a moment—quiet, together—until the clock on her nightstand reminds us it's already after four.

I blink. "We should probably go."

Aliza straightens up, nodding. "Yeah. You need to print that masterpiece."

I close the laptop, grab the charger, and follow her downstairs to the kitchen. Her dad helps us find the printer, and after a few clicks and a small paper jam panic, the speech comes sliding out—two crisp pages that feel heavier than they should.

I tuck them into a folder and glance over at Aliza. She's watching me, smiling like she knows I've just crossed some invisible finish line.

"You ready?" she asks.

I take a deep breath. "Yeah. I think I am."

We head to her car, making our way back to the ceremony. The drive is quiet—but not the kind that feels heavy or tense. It's the kind of quiet that means everything's been said. Now it's just time to live it.

Her hand finds mine somewhere along the way, and neither of us lets go.

We don't talk, but we don't have to. There's something grounding in the way our fingers stay laced together—like we're anchoring each other for what comes next.

By the time we pull into the lot behind the football field, it's already packed. Students are adjusting caps and gowns, parents are snapping pictures from every angle, and teachers are handing out last-minute instructions while trying (and mostly failing) not to cry.

Aliza gives my hand a squeeze before we climb out, and I carry that small strength with me as we step into the crowd.

Just past the registration table, we spot her parents waving us over. They're standing near a row of folding chairs—her mom holding a small bouquet of wildflowers, her dad with his camera already slung around his neck.

"There's our graduates!" her dad calls out, grinning.

Before we can even respond, I hear a familiar laugh—Elliot's—and then he's there with Erica, both dressed in their caps and gowns, walking over with his grandparents in tow. His grandma hugs Aliza gently, then pulls me in like I've always belonged.

And then I see them—my parents. My mom's eyes are already misty, tissues clutched in one hand. My dad stands beside her with a proud, quiet smile that says more than words ever could.

We spend the next few minutes taking pictures—every combination we can think of.

Aliza with her parents.
Me with mine.
The four of us—me, Aliza, Elliot, and Erica—grinning like we're trying to freeze this moment forever.

A goofy one. A serious one.
One where Aliza rests her head on my shoulder, and I know I'll remember the weight of it for the rest of my life.

And in the middle of it all, no one says it out loud—but I think we all feel it:

We made it.

Chapter 37 –Confetti and Keys

The sun hangs low but golden as we gather behind the school. A soft breeze rustles the line of folding chairs set out on the field, and the metal bleachers gleam with movement—parents waving, cameras flashing, little siblings holding handmade signs.

We're given directions by teachers who've mostly stopped pretending to be in charge. There's too much energy. Too much emotion. Too much of everything.

We line up by alphabet, caps adjusted a hundred times over. The gowns feel too big or too small, and nobody can quite figure out which side the tassel is supposed to start on.

The sun was already warming the football field, and we were lined up just outside the stadium gates—caps adjusted, nerves buzzing, a hundred conversations happening at once.

I stepped a little away from the group, needing a second to breathe. The weight of everything—this day, the speech I still hadn't practiced out loud, the fact that it was actually ending—pressed against my ribs like a held breath.

That's when Mrs. Carson appeared beside me, clipboard in hand, looking every bit like she belonged there—organized, calm, quietly keeping the chaos in check.

But she wasn't checking anything. Not really.

Her eyes found mine before she spoke.

"I heard you're giving the closing remarks."

I nodded, fidgeting with the edge of my gown. "Yeah. Kind of a last-minute thing."

She smiled, soft and certain. "I can't think of anyone better."

I tried to smile back, but it felt tight. "I'm still not even sure what I'm going to say."

"You've already said it," she replied. "In your writing. In how you show up. In how far you've come."

She paused, then added, "That narrative you turned in—about Jessi, the zoo, the red light… I just want you to know, I still think about it. You didn't just write a memory. You gave her life on the page. That kind of writing stays with people."

I felt my throat tighten.

"I didn't think it was anything special," I admitted.

She shook her head. "It was honest. That's what made it powerful. You've carried so much this year, and still, you found the courage to put it into words. That matters, Patrick. You matter."

Her voice wasn't overly sentimental. It was steady. Grounded.

True.

I looked at her then—really looked.

And realized something I hadn't said out loud.

I'd always believed her.

Even when I couldn't believe in myself.

I move back to the line.

Aliza stands two spots ahead of me, near the front. Elliot and Erica are further back, joking with the kids next to them. I glance around, soaking it in.

We're walking out.

Into something new.

The music starts—a familiar instrumental that echoes across the field, soft and a little shaky through the old sound system. A few cheers rise from the crowd as we begin the slow walk out from behind the school and onto the football field.

Step by step, the line moves forward.

Rows of chairs stretch across the grass, the sun warming our shoulders as we file in. It smells like fresh-cut grass, sunscreen, and something else I can't quite name—nostalgia, maybe. Or the start of goodbye.

I find my seat, two down from Aliza, and glance into the crowd.

There's Mom, already dabbing her eyes with a tissue.

The principal steps up to the microphone. "Good evening, and welcome to the commencement ceremony for the Black Hills High School graduating class…"

The applause is polite. Nervous. It's really happening.

A few speeches come and go. Faculty members. Counselors. The kind of advice people give at graduations and forget the next day.

Then it's Aliza's turn.

She steps up to the podium, smooth and composed. Her voice carries clear and steady across the stadium. Confident. But still completely her.

"Four years ago, we walked into this school as strangers. We leave it tonight as something more—because we have shaped one another. Through joy, through pain, through every impossible test."

She pauses to look around at all of us.

"Someone once told me that the hardest goodbyes are the ones that were never supposed to happen. But I've come to believe that the hardest goodbyes… are also the most important. Because they mean we had something worth losing."

A hush falls over the crowd.

"We are not the same people we were. And that's a good thing. We are stronger. Softer. Braver. And more than ready for what comes next."

She closes with a quiet thank you, and the audience erupts in applause.

I catch her eyes as she returns to her seat, and she smiles—not just proud, but sure. Of herself. Of me. Of us.

The names begin—slow at first, then settling into a rhythm.

"Jameson, Olivia."
"Liu, Marcus."
"Martinez, Selena."

"Vasquez, Jonah."
"Wells, Caroline."

"Woolstenhulme, Isaac"
"Zirker, Grace."

The last of the alphabet.

Applause rises and fades, again and again, like waves pulling back from shore. I glance toward the podium and see Principal Powell stepping forward, adjusting the mic.

Here it comes.

He clears his throat, looking out over the crowd.

"Traditionally, I would offer a few final words to close out the ceremony," he says. "But tonight… I think someone else has something worth saying."

He pauses, letting the weight of it settle.

"This young man has faced challenges most of us can't imagine. And yet, he's stood back up—again and again—with quiet strength, resilience, and grace. It is my honor to introduce our student speaker for the evening… Patrick Schwartz."

Applause begins, and I stand slowly.

My legs feel like they've forgotten how to work. My heartbeat's in my throat. But I walk.

Step by step, across the grass, toward the podium.

I glance toward the front row—toward her.

Aliza meets my eyes and gives the smallest nod. It's nothing flashy. Just… *I'm here.*

I hold onto that.

I shake Principal Powell's hand, step behind the mic, and look out at the crowd. It's a sea of faces—parents, teachers, neighbors. The whole town, it feels like.

I take a breath.

Then I begin.

"Well… hi."

A few chuckles echo from the crowd. My voice wavers just a little.

"I… uh… I found out about three hours ago that I'd be speaking tonight, so if this goes sideways, just smile and clap anyway."

More laughter. It helps. I let myself breathe again.

"I'm not up here because I'm the best student. Or the best athlete. Or because I ran for senior class president. I didn't."

Another beat.

"I'm here because this year almost broke me. And somehow… I'm still standing."

I glance down at my pages, at the lines I scratched out and rewrote in a rush an hour ago.

"1 year ago, I was in a car accident. I walked away. But my sister, Jessi… didn't."

The crowd falls silent. I find Mom in the front row. Her hands are clutched tight around a tissue. Dad's arm is around her, steady and sure.

"I lost the person who knew me better than anyone else. The one who saw me—even when I was invisible to everyone else."

I swallow. My throat tightens, but I keep going.

"And in the months after that, I started disappearing, too. Not physically—but emotionally. I shut people out. I convinced myself that grief and guilt were just who I was now."

I pause.

"Then this fall, at Homecoming… I snapped. And the mask I'd been wearing shattered in front of the whole school."

There are murmurs in the crowd. Everyone remembers.

"I thought that moment would define me forever. That I'd become a cautionary tale—some kid who broke under pressure and couldn't recover."

I let that hang in the air.

"But I didn't stay broken. I didn't stay invisible."

I look out at my classmates, scanning the rows of caps and gowns, faces I once tried to avoid.

"I started to let people in. Even when it was hard. Even when I didn't trust they'd stay. I started to heal."

I glance at Elliot and Erica. I see Aliza, steady in her seat, giving me that look—the one that says *I see you. Keep going.*

And just behind the crowd—just for a second—I see a silhouette standing near the edge of the field.

Red hoodie. Hands in the pockets. Head tilted like she's listening.

Jessi.

She's not real. I know that. But something about her being there—just there—fills me with a quiet kind of peace.

I stand a little taller.

"I still miss her. Every single day. I still carry what happened. But it doesn't own me anymore."

My voice steadies.

"I've learned that grief is a long, winding road—and not every goodbye gets closure. Some stay messy. Some stay painful. And some…"

I pause, looking toward the sky now lit with soft gold.

"Some goodbyes stay unfinished."

I see Aliza's eyes widen just slightly. She knows what that means.

"But maybe that's okay. Maybe the most important part isn't finishing the goodbye. Maybe it's learning how to live in spite of it. How to carry the love forward."

The silence that follows is warm. Present. I let it linger.

"Tonight, we close a chapter of our lives. But we also begin something new. Whether you're going off to college, moving across the country, or staying right here—what you do next matters. How you live matters."

I take a final breath.

"I'll always carry the weight of what happened. But I don't carry it alone anymore. And I don't let it define me."

My voice softens.

"That's what this year taught me. That's what Jessi taught me."

A pause. The wind picks up, gentle across the mic.

"Thank you."

I step back from the microphone, the words still echoing across the field.

For a moment, no one moves. No one breathes.

Then the crowd rises to their feet.

Applause breaks out—loud and full and rising like a wave. I hear someone whistle. Someone else shout my name. But mostly, it's just the sound of people *seeing me*—really seeing me—for the first time not as the kid who broke… but as the one who rebuilt.

I return to my seat. Aliza reaches for my hand, her eyes full of tears and pride and something soft I can't quite name.

Principal Powell steps back up to the mic.

"Class of twenty-twenty-six," he says, beaming. "On the count of three…"

We all stand. Our hands move to the tops of our caps.

"One…"

A hush spreads.

"Two…"

I look around—at Elliot, at Erica, at Aliza, at the sky.

"Three!"

Caps fly into the air like fireworks. A rain of fabric and tassels and joy.

Confetti cannons blast from both sides of the stage—gold and silver filling the sunlight like something out of a dream.

We cheer. We scream. We laugh.

And for the first time in a long time, I feel *light.*

Free.

Not from the memory. Not from Jessi.

But from the fear that I wouldn't survive all of this.

Because I did.

The confetti still floats in the air, catching in the breeze like tiny pieces of sunlight. I'm standing near the edge of the field, my cap long lost to the sky, when I feel a hand on my shoulder.

I turn.

It's Mom.

Her arms are already around me before I can say a word. She holds me like she's trying to memorize the shape of me all over again—like this moment is something she's been waiting for, too.

"I'm so proud of you," she whispers into my ear, her voice shaking. "You did it, Patrick."

"I didn't do it alone," I say, my voice catching. "But… thank you."

When she steps back, Dad is right behind her. He doesn't say anything at first. Just pulls me into a hug—the kind that's solid and real and everything I never thought I'd get back. When he lets go, he claps a hand on my shoulder and reaches into his pocket.

He pulls out a small silver key ring and holds it out to me. "You'll need this at the University of Colorado next year," he says, a proud grin tugging at the corner of his mouth. "It's out in the parking lot. Nothing fancy, but it runs smooth, and it's all yours."

I just stare at it.

A car.

A future.

A gift I never expected—from a man I never thought would look at me the way he's looking at me now.

I take the keys slowly, my fingers closing around the cool metal. "Dad…"

He shakes his head, brushing off whatever apology or disbelief I might try to offer. "You earned it. Every bit of this—you earned."

Aliza steps forward then, her hand finding mine. Mom turns and wraps her in a hug, like she's been part of this family all along. "Thank you," Mom says, her voice thick. "For standing by him."

Aliza smiles through the emotion in her eyes. "He's the one who held on."

Dad leans in and gives her a one-armed squeeze too. "You're part of the reason he's here. I hope you know that."

We all stand there for a moment, caught in a quiet pocket of sunlight and love, the kind that feels stitched together from too many broken pieces to count.

And maybe that's what makes it beautiful.

Maybe this is what healing really looks like—not erasing the pain, but learning to live with it in full color. Bright. Unapologetic. Honest.

As we walk off the field together—Aliza on one side, Mom and Dad on the other—I realize something.

I didn't just survive.

I arrived.

And this time… I'm not leaving anything unsaid.

After the crowd thins and the hugs slow, I spot it parked near the edge of the lot—a small, silver commuter car, clean and modest. Nothing flashy. But it's mine.

I make my way toward it, graduation cap still in hand, fingers curling around the keys Dad gave me.

For a second, I just stand there.

It's the first time I've sat behind the wheel since the accident.

The first time since everything changed.

My chest tightens. My fingers hover over the door handle, trembling just enough to notice. What if the fear comes back? What if I freeze?

But then I remember Jessi's voice from the dream. *"You didn't kill me. You loved me. And now… you have to love yourself enough to live."*

I breathe in. I unlock the door.

The seat hugs me like it's been waiting. I slide the key into the ignition and turn it. The engine hums to life—steady, unshaken. And with it, something inside me settles.

This is different.

This is new.

I shift into gear, pull out slowly, and let the wheels carry me forward—not just toward Aliza's house, but toward whatever comes next.

Chapter 38 – Chasing What Matters

The sky is streaked with fading gold when I pull into Aliza's driveway, following her back to her house.

The backyard is already full—classmates laughing around the fire pit, music drifting softly from the speaker near the porch, someone balancing a plate of cupcakes like a waiter at a five-star restaurant.

It smells like toasted marshmallows, grilled burgers, and summer.

I spot Elliot near the fire, tossing a marshmallow to Erica, who catches it midair like it's an Olympic sport. Aliza and I join them, our shoulders brushing as we sit on the old patio bench that creaks every time someone shifts.

We talk. We laugh. We breathe.

There's no pressure now. No fear. Just warmth and ash and the slow hum of goodbye.

For the first time, I don't feel like I'm racing to hold onto this moment. I'm just *in it.*

After a while, Aliza tugs my hand.

"Come with me," she says, rising to her feet.

She leads me past the edge of the crowd, to the far side of the yard where the string lights fade into dark, and the stars finally get their say.

We stop near the fence, just the two of us.

She looks up at me, eyes reflecting firelight and something deeper.

"You did so good tonight," she says softly. "I don't think anyone will forget that speech."

I start to respond, but she shakes her head. "Don't downplay it. You were honest. Brave. Everything people needed to hear."

I look down at her, hand still in mine.

"Couldn't have done it without you."

She smirks. "I know."

A pause. Then she exhales.

"There's something I've been wanting to tell you. But I didn't want it to distract you before graduation."

My heart slows.

"I turned down UCLA," she says, her voice steady. "I declined the scholarship."

My breath catches.

"What?"

She nods. "It was hard. But the more I thought about it… the more I realized what I want right now isn't sunshine and celebrities. It's *this.* You. Us. So I accepted a spot at Colorado. I'll be cheering there in the fall."

I stare at her, stunned.

"You're serious?"

"I am," she says. "Our next adventure continues together."

And just like that—any leftover fear, any lingering shadow, melts in her light.

I pull her in and wrap my arms around her. She leans into my chest like she belongs there.

And maybe she always has.

The fire pops behind us. Laughter echoes across the yard.

Somewhere, a song we all know plays quietly into the night.

And for the first time in forever, I'm not thinking about what I lost.

I'm thinking about what comes next.

www.ingramcontent.com/pod-product-compliance
Lightning Source LLC
Chambersburg PA
CBHW050306110726
47899CB00007B/2133
9798993680101